KEPRESSNG ANTHOLOGY PRIZE
VINE 2022

Notes on Love
&
Other Stories

KEP

First published by Kemka Ezinwo Press
No. 79 Udo Otung Ubo Street
Uyo, Akwa Ibom State.
Nigeria.
KEP has no control over or responsibility for any author or third-party websites referred to in or on this book.

978 978 999 285 0 (Hardback)
978 191 637 108 8 (Ebook)
978 191 637 109 5 (Paperback)

A CIP catalogue record for this book is available from the National Library of Nigeria and the British Library.

Cover credit: James – **www.goonwrite.com**
Illustration Credit: Chimele Ezinwo of Chigirl Arts

Welcome to 2022.

Due to the success of the maiden edition of the KEPRESSNG ANTHOLOGY PRIZE 2021, we decided to increase the number of competitions we'll have every given year. For ease, we created unique titles for the 2022 competitions to negate the need to use KEPRESSNG ANTHOLOGY PRIZE 2022. (We will use it for some time of course). The titles are:

1.   VINE
2.   LILY
3.   JUVENILE
4.   OAK

All competitions are limited to five thousand words except JUVENILE which has a ten thousand word maximum. This competition, we hope, will remain constant as an annual event for the next five years before we move it to a bi-annual event.

For the VINE competition, we picked the theme Love and, or Solidarity. It's our way of thanking the African Literary world for never giving up. And that we stand in solidarity with the growth of literacy in Africa and African literature.

The stories married well with the theme. They embrace love and solidarity in unforgettable, vivid and sometimes humorous alignment with escapades which include haunting stories as in a sister's protection, finding love in enemy lines, falling in love with a false representation, a mother's confusion on where her loyalty should lie, the marred lines between love and hate and the general fear of falling back into that state of unrest.

CONTENTS

LOVE IN BLOOM

♥

Chidinma Vivian Nnalue

Ugonne was just like the first syllable of her name. Ugo - Glory. Or eagle. And she was just as glorious, just as graceful as the eagle. She was extraordinary like that king of birds. Except that almost everyone who knew her age thought something was wrong with her.

For instance, why was she not married at thirty-five? Why was there no man in her life? But it wasn't that there had never been a man. There just wasn't any man who had shown any romantic interest in her in the last two years.

Two years since she had seen pictures of Nwokedi in a bathtub cradling a grinning toothless baby. Pictures that Nwokedi's sister, who was also Ugonne's closest friend, had hidden from her. Asa had said she had kept quiet because she didn't want to hurt Ugonne. But then, one of those pictures had also been Asa's screen saver, and there was no doubt that she was in on the matter.

That day, Ugonne had slid Nwokedi's ring out of her finger and flushed it down the toilet. She would never be caught going out with lying, cheating bastards anymore. Two years later, she still hadn't gone out with a lying, cheating bastard, nor with any other type of man for that matter. Only now, she worried that the decision she had taken, with her heart as the only witness, had somehow found its way to the surface and was announcing to everyone that this one was a *'no go area'* even though she was now ready for a relationship.

Ugonne was tired of seeing pyjama-clad families all over Instagram every other Christmas. She was tired of her mother asking her when she would get married. And of her grandmother asking her what the problem was. She wished she could ask them what the problem was too. She wished she could ask why their own husbands had left them to care for their children alone.

She was tired of people responding to her WhatsApp status with, 'Don't worry, I will come and eat rice at your own wedding too' whenever she posted photos from weddings she attended. She was tired of people who chirped that maybe her not being married yet was a spiritual matter, and she needed deliverance. But most of all, she was ready to fall in love again. She was ready for love, companionship, and the beauty of having her own man. A really good man.

The door slid open, rousing her from her thoughts. It was her secretary, Tersoo. When would the girl learn to knock? Ugonne wondered. And she would always punctuate the oversight with 'Sorry ma.' 'Why don't you just do the right thing and skip the sorry?'. That was what was on the tip of

Ugonne's tongue, but she held back. It was one of her New Year's resolutions: to say no evil. To really be a better person and show people grace. She knew she could be hard to get along with. Her former friend, Asa, had even gone about telling everyone that Ugonne was too uptight, which was why her brother had left her. But Ugonne knew that both brother and sister were only really foolish. She turned her mind to the present. And to the figure standing in front of her.

"Yes?" she asked, a smile parting her lips. She hoped the smile didn't look as forced as the little voice in her head told her it did.

"Sorry ma, there's someone here to see you."

"Oh, okay. Did you ask for the person's name?" she asked, her hand fiddling with the brooch on her dress.

"Ermm, ma, he said his name is Yakub. I think Jacob. I'm not sure, ma."

"Hmmm," Ugonne mused. She didn't know any Yakub. But a Jacob. *Wait, could it be?* "Okay, let him in," she finally said.

The door opened then, and it was just the person she had imagined it would be.

"Heyyyy," he cooed loudly.

"Ah, Jakes, come in. Come in." Ugonne inhaled sharply. "My secretary said you were Jacob, and I was racking my head." She gave a small laugh before motioning him to a seat. "It's so good to see you." She cleared her throat softly. "Wow! When we talked yesterday, I had no idea you were anywhere near town not to talk of you knowing my office."

Jakes laughed, throwing his head back before replying, "I mostly go by Jacob these days. And hey, I have my ways of knowing things."

Yeah, you sure do, Ugonne thought before catching herself and waving the thought away. Here was Jakes. In the flesh. It was still a surprise to her that evening when he had called her saying that he had seen in the class group that it was her birthday. Ugonne had been surprised to hear that anyone had cared to celebrate her birthday in the group after she had exited some months earlier. Too many *WhatsApp* groups, she had said. And besides, there was nothing happening in the group anyway. Jakes had sent her a birthday message on *WhatsApp* after collecting her phone number from one of the group admins.

There was an awkward silence in the room.

Why was he here?

"I moved to Lagos about a year ago," he offered as if he had started to read her thoughts. "This city is crazy. I still cannot deal. How do you Lagosians cope? I prefer Bauchi, honestly."

Ugonne wanted to laugh. It was a question she had heard one too many times from Lagos *newbies*.

"Well, we just cope," she replied with a shrug. She was used to Lagos. Including all its *wahala* and had even developed a thick skin. "You mentioned Bauchi. I never pictured you as a cool, tucked away from the city kinda guy. You've been living in Bauchi?" Ugonne saw his face twitch with emotion.

Was that sadness? Ah, I hope I hadn't opened up any wounds.

"Well, let's say I play it cool these days," he said and laughed.

Ugonne knew he was back to his bubbly self, the same personality that had earned him quite the reputation with some girls in their school days.

"So I was thinking, Ugo," he started. "I know this is rather short notice, but if you don't have any plans for Valentine's, maybe we could go out, catch up..." he trailed off.

Jakes had said, 'catch up', as though there was ever a time when they were close. But she replied with, "Oh no. I mean, no, I don't have plans. Sounds cool."

"Great," he said, his face beaming with a smile.

Ugonne fixed her gaze on his cheeks. *Is that a dimple?*

"Thank you. I'll leave you to it," Jakes said, pointing to the pile of paperwork sitting on her desk.

Ugonne gave a faint smile.

"I just didn't want to tell you this over the phone, and besides, it's been so long. I also wanted to see your face."

Hmm, Ugonne thought before saying, "Awww, thanks."

Jakes stood up, all six feet of him. He was every inch as handsome as he had been since she last saw him ten years ago. That was before he had disappeared, and the stories had started to fly around. Stories about him and other cultists like him fleeing the school with nothing but the shirts on their backs. That was in those days when the school authorities had made the campus too hot for any cultists to remain. What was Jakes's story now? Ugo wondered. Also, what was that twinkle she saw dancing in his eyes?

She stood up and moved towards him. But before she could stretch a hand for a shake, he wrapped her in a small hug. Ugonne managed to stop herself from stiffening and instead hugged him back.

That was fast. She soon found herself breathing in his cologne. It had been so long since she hugged a man. Any man. And did this feel good? Yes. Even though she tried to deny it.

★★★

"Hey, Ugonne."

"Hi!" Ugonne called

"Ready?" Jakes asked into the phone.

"Just a few more minutes. Where are you?"

"Admiralty Way. I should be at yours in less than fifteen."

"Wow. Folks usually find it hard locating my place the first time."

He didn't reply, but she could picture a smile playing on his lips.

"Okay, till you come," Ugonne said before

hanging up. What was she doing? she asked herself, tracing the curve of her lips with a pencil. In the past few days, Jakes, or as he now called himself, Jacob, had been so vested in her, calling her, sending text messages and even earlier today, he had sent a bunch of roses to her office with a note tucked in that read:

For Ugo,
More beautiful than a thousand roses in bloom.
Will you be my Val?

Ugonne had found herself smiling like a love-struck teenager. She knew there was a lot she still needed to know about Jakes. Only, she didn't want to rush things. Just take it slow. After all, he hadn't asked her out yet.

She heard the gate open, and her heart did a couple of flip-flops. She smoothened invisible creases from her dress and checked herself out one last time before heading for the door.

Jakes had just placed his hand on the doorbell, ready to press the bell, when a beautiful woman in a red gown appeared. She looked...

What was the word? Exquisite? For want of a better word, he would go with that. They both walked to his car, chatting all the way there and Jakes held open the door for his date. Ugonne slipped into the vehicle, mouthing her thanks.

***

It had been a lovely evening at Oaks and Hearts. The

place was beautiful, and the ocean air wafted in from the view overlooking the ocean had soothed Ugonne's near anxious nerves. She and Jakes had talked about a lot of things. She had learnt that he moved on to a private university after the cultism issue, but that was after seeing a therapist for one year. The experience seemed to have both shattered and changed him, especially as his best friend, Okey, had died in a cult clash. But Ugonne decided not to mention Okey. She instead allowed him to tease her about always *doing shakara for him* then, even though he had been all sweet on her for the longest time.

Ugonne peeled off her clothes and dropped into bed as soon as she entered her room. She knew that Jakes would call but she wasn't sure she'd be awake when he did. It had been a richly rewarding and way more satisfying evening than she had imagined. She soon drifted into a sweet sleep with images of Jakes filling her head.

Godiya was calling again.

What does she want this time? Jakes wondered. It was only 8 o'clock, and he had thought he would lie in a little longer after the long night with Ugonne. They hadn't left the restaurant until past eleven p.m. They were some of the last people remaining, and it was getting too late; he would have wanted them to stay for longer. He answered the phone when it started to ring for the second time.

"Hello, Godiya."

"*Toh!* They said you've started to carry women in Lagos already. Well, I'd have said you will tell the judge how come you're doing that when we haven't fully been divorced, but your errors are forgiving. I'm not up for that divorce agreement again *oo*. I've changed my mind," she blurted out all at once.

Jakes was beyond stunned. Who was this woman, really? How did she know there was a woman in Lagos? And wasn't that an assumption? Because she was capable of assuming many things. Those same assumptions had led her to think he didn't want her anymore, and then the quarrels followed.

Jakes had gotten married to Godiya right after his NYSC service year. He knew he didn't love her. But what they lacked in love, they made up for in the bedroom, igniting fires that a hundred rivers could hardly douse. And that had been okay until two years had passed without a child, and Godiya had started to transfer all the angst her mother laid on her over the absence of a child on him. It had been constant nags and accusations and complaints until he had gotten a transfer to Lagos, and when she refused to come with him, he decided on a divorce. Good riddance, in his opinion.

"What I want is simple," Godiya started to say, then paused for effect. "I want to come to Lagos. I want to try having a child again. I want it to be yours. Me, I can't give my body to another man o. You started the thing, and you will finish it. Just give me a child, *gaskiya,* and I will get off your back."

Jakes could hardly say a word. He just clicked the end button on the call and lay on the bed again, struggling in vain to return to his sleep.

★★★

After Valentine's Day, Ugonne and Jakes had had dinner together again, and he had slid his arm toward her side of the table, held her hands and remarked on how soft they felt, how she had the hands of an *ajebó* who had never worked a day.

"I wish," Ugonne had said.

He had started to caress her hands with his lips then, pelting them with small kisses before finally asking, "Obim. Can I call you Obim?" He was like a high school lad who had just discovered that something could be stirred in his heart for a girl.

Ugonne let out a chuckle. "Where did you hear that?"

"Ah! This one you're laughing like this, is 'Obim' not what I think it is?" he asked, a playful smile on his lips.

"It is," Ugonne replied, laughing. "Only that I wanted to know where you'd heard it."

"Well, it's everywhere. That's the title of one Timi Dakolo song *nau, abi.* And besides that, it just feels so right calling you that. My heart. I don't have a heart anymore. I think I've given it to you. Take all of me, baby." Laughing, he continued, "And hey, I'm not joking. It just feels like being right here with you is the only place I should ever be."

He hoped he hadn't ever used that line on Godiya. But then, it wasn't even a line, he told himself. It was just how he felt. There was a time he had felt a semblance of safety with Godiya. Actually, he had really felt safe. But that was before the nagging. With Ugonne, he felt more than safe – he was home.

"To be honest, Ugo, I didn't realise how much I had wanted us until I saw a picture of you that day on the class group and everyone celebrating you."

"I wonder who even added me to that group *sef seeing* as I never graduated with the rest of you all." He laughed, and Ugonne told herself that she could spend all her life listening to that sound. "I want you in my life. You probably already know I have a ton of history. Shitty history to be precise. If you'd just give me a chance, I'll make you a very happy woman. Okay, scratch that, I'll do all I can to make you happy. And I truly believe that my life would be so much better because of you."

Ugonne gave a small nod before opening her mouth to say, "Yes. Yes, I will be your girlfriend if that's what you're asking."

***

The address is 264, Biodun Falomo. That's what I put

into the app *nau*. I don't know the description o. Just follow the map Oga *abeg.*', Godiya said.

Godiya had been in Lagos for a day now. First, because of her friend, Ibukun's wedding and second, because of Jakes. Since that day when he had hung up after she talked about having his child, she had been unable to reach him. He didn't return calls, didn't reply to her texts and when she reached him on WhatsApp, it took days for him to reply. The driver turned into a street.

Honestly, Godiya hadn't wanted to bother Bimpe with her marital issues. If she could still say she had a marriage. She consoled herself with the knowledge that Jakes had never been able to resist her. He used to find some solace, some comfort from all his worries at her bosom, and she was ready to satisfy him again. Every man could find comfort in his wife's bosom. The Bible had been right about that. Or was it some post she had read on Cosmopolitan? She tended to mix these things up these days.

Bimpe had told her to fight for her marriage. Or did she say, 'look for someone else to get you laid and stop being religious, girl'? Godiya couldn't tell exactly what her friend had said. But if Bimpe had guessed that Godiya needed to get laid, then she had been right. It had been a year already. One whole year without a man. Still, she could never think of giving her body to another man. It was Jakes or no one else.

She had been foolish to sever what little connection they had had even though it wasn't love. Maybe once Jakes saw her, his passion for her would be rekindled and they would be just like old times. She would hold on to the only fragment of intimacy they had ever shared. It was little but she would have to make do with that little.

★★★

The security man, Cheta, had called to tell Jakes that there was someone at the gate asking to see him. The person didn't say her name and Jakes told Cheta to let her in but when Godiya walked into the house, he knew he had made a mistake.

"My husband. *Ya kake*-How are you doing?" she asked, moving to hug him.

He didn't stop her as he was too stunned to speak.

"*Toh*, this place is beautiful o. *Wallahi*, you've always had good taste." Her eyes roamed the beautifully decorated sitting room while her hands clasped one of his.

He tore his hand off before asking, "Godiya, what are you doing here? You know it's over for us. So, don't come in here acting like all is well and good."

"*Haba,*" she said and moved to recline on a sofa before continuing, "I know you've never really loved me. I think you could learn to. Babe, please give us another chance. I believe this time too I can carry your child. Maybe a child is what we need."

At that, Jakes scoffed before saying, "I'm not having this discussion with you, Godiya. You already know. I'm heading out. By the time I get back, you should no longer be here. Don't make me have to call security."

And with that, he strode out of the house, shutting the door with a bang before collecting himself and wondering why he was letting himself lose it on her account.

★★★

Ugonne had never been happier in her whole life. She was sure of this. She was even sure she had started to glow, what with all the compliments she had started to get lately. They could continue to look and talk, but she was Jakes' alone, and he was hers.

He had introduced her to his circle of friends, and every other month, they had a get-together where they relaxed, let off steam and enjoy friendship and companionship. With all of these, Ugonne was starting to think that this was really her year. God had not only sent her a loving man but had also given her a bunch of friends; a community full of love and support. And there was Lolu. Her phone started to vibrate just then. Talk of the devil, she said, smiling.

"Hey, girlfriend."

"Hi, boo."

'Where you dey?"

"The office. *Waddup?*"

"No o. Nothing. I say make I greet you. It's a slow business day. So, I said, let me say hello. I missed you guys at the last brunch, everything okay?"

"Yes, we're good o. *Le boo* said he had a busy day and he had to work Saturday."

"We'll be at the next one, *no worry*. As you've refused to come see me nau. And don't beg me o. *I no dey come see you again unless you come my place.*" Lolu started to laugh. "No worry, I go surprise you."

21

"Abeg, chill," Ugonne started to say. "Hey babes, someone just came into the shop. Let me talk to you later, okay?"

"Ah, see now o. I carry blessings. *I don bring customer now now now. No wahala.* God bless your work today, dear."

"Amen," Lolu answered before laughing and saying, "My prophetess. Oya nau bye."

"Bye," Ugonne echoed.

Lolu started to answer the client. As she did, she thought about her friend, Ugonne. About how she had heard the day before that Jakes had a wife. Or was it that his wife was back? Was that the reason why he hadn't been around last week? Only she couldn't tell Ugonne what she had heard and suspected to be true. How could she? She was no gossip. But even as she thought of it, she wondered what would hurt more. Her silence or her revelation. All she could do was hope. And she hoped that Ugonne wouldn't end up being hurt by this man whom she loved with all her heart.

★★★

It had all happened so fast. Jakes had returned that night, not bothering to check if Godiya had left and sometime during his sleep, someone had slid into bed with him. Before he knew it, Godiya's hands were all over him and he felt paralysed to do anything. He had forgotten everything else and focused on his need. Focused on the fact that he had missed the workings of a woman's hands on his body. Then they had both glided through the clouds and come crashing down again before he realised what he had done. Before he realised his body had betrayed him, and he had betrayed the woman he claimed to love, Ugonne.

Jakes had sent Godiya away the next day while she continued to scream and pound on his gate saying that he couldn't use her just like that. But Jakes was only thinking of Ugonne. Telling her what had happened might just mean the end. She had once shared her dreams of a stable family with him. She didn't have that growing up. And Jakes knew he was far from stable. Not with his history. Except if things like these blurred out when you started to do the right thing. But then now, he had betrayed her trust.

How do I tell her what I have done? he thought. It had been three days since he had last called. The only time he had sent her a message in recent times was even a reply to her WhatsApp message where she had been asking if he was okay. He said he was. But he knew he couldn't keep punishing himself this way. And punishing her more. He wished that the divorce process would hasten.

He would call Ugonne. He wondered if it was a good time, but he called still. She picked up on the first ring.

"Hey Obim," he spoke into the phone.

"Hi! How are you?" she asked. This one he was

calling her Obim today, was he back to himself? she wondered. He had a lot of explaining to do. But first, she would enjoy the sound of his voice filling her ears. *God, whatever you did to bring him back, thank you oo*, she thought.

"Can we do dinner tonight? I've missed you so much," he said.

She wanted to say, 'Ehn, then why didn't you call since? What really happened with you *sef* because you just *ghosted* me. And nothing I did to bring you out of your shell worked.' Instead, she decided not to say that. They would see and they would talk. Ah, she loved this man so much. It had taken a lot for her not to run to him asking what she had done. Of course, she had asked but she could have begged him even though she wasn't sure she had done anything wrong.

"Sure," she answered into the phone wondering how many minutes of silence had stretched between them before she agreed.

★★★

Ugonne was dressed in a strapless blue gown and was the very picture of beauty. Jakes stood to hug her and drew out a chair for her afterwards. He only wondered whether she would want him back after she heard what he had to say.

Quite the place. Must have cost a lot.

It was fancier than anywhere Jakes had ever taken

her. She wondered if he was going to pop the question. But then again, she thought, 'Not so fast.' They had only been dating for four months, including the brief interval when he had just gone quiet on her. It was not too early because she had heard of people who dated and got married in a really short time. Only she wanted to get to know Jakes better. She didn't want to make a mistake.

Meanwhile, seated across from her, Jakes was fighting a battle. Should he tell her? Should he not? He couldn't afford to keep any more secrets. He cleared his throat before saying, 'Ugo, I've never told you this, but I was married."

He saw her shift in her seat.

He continued, "I say 'was' because I am currently going through a divorce. It's just taking longer than I thought these things take." He waited for her to say something, anything, and when she didn't, he continued. "My ex-wife," he paused and swallowed. "She was here two weeks ago. And we had sex."

He knit all ten fingers of his hands. "I wish I could say I didn't know what I was doing. I did. I knew how I could never resist her in the past, yet I didn't send her away. She said she wanted a baby. I don't know," he trailed off before continuing again. "She said she wanted us back together. I don't know how I allowed myself fall into this, but I should have told you from the onset. I am so sorry. I'm so sorry I kept it all from you. I'm sorry I betrayed you this way. I was..."

He paused and his eyes clouded with pain. "You know my history but maybe, you don't know the full of it and I promise not to hide anything from you again."

He knew he was saying a lot of things. He was saying more than he usually did. But from now on, he intended to start talking. No more half-truths or silence. He was sure that Godiya would be back. He knew they hadn't used protection that night, but he really hoped she would not get pregnant. After all, they had tried many times in their two-year-old marriage, but she hadn't been pregnant even once.

He decided not to bother with that. He was only waiting for the woman seated in front of him to say something. The silence was much harder to bear. The room was dimly lit, and Jakes wondered if what he had seen drop to her cheek was a tear.

"God, what have I done?" he asked himself. But then it was only some seconds more before she reached for his hand and said:

"If you'll fight for us, then I'll fight by your side."

Jakes was beyond thrilled. God had dealt him more than he deserved. *Gosh, this woman.*

Ugonne looked at the man seated in front of her. She still had questions. Lots of them. But for now, she would put that aside and stay by his side. She continued holding on and gave his hand a reassuring squeeze. They had a long way to go but she would take the first wild step with him, with love prodding them on.

Chidinma Vivian Nnalue is a short story writer living in Lagos, Nigeria. She loves journals, would love to explore places and believes no one should get tired of 'licking ice-cream'. She hopes to write more stories about Nigeria and Nigerians. Presently, she takes one day at a time mastering how to thrive in the bustling city of Lagos.

THE S.O.S.

♥

Aninoritse Ejuliuwa

She called it, *Ajenirun*, this thing that was following him. She said his great-great-grandfather offended it, defied its orders and went into the arms of a ravishing woman who descended from a lineage with a much darker offence. She sprinkled and smeared what had the colour and consistency of talcum powder but smelt like rotten eggs on his palm, which she had seized in her ringed claws.

He gagged.

She cackled.

Goose pimples covered him. "It will not rest until it wastes you all completely," she eyeballed him, "and poverty is just one of its means." Then she smiled, a smile that stretched her reed-thin, coal-black mouth to an impossible extent.

"But I can help you."

Wind gushed in and rattled the cluster of tiny mirrors and cowries hanging from the stooped, ceiling-less, rusted zinc roofing.

"It is already upon you, but I like you. I will help you."

***

In the rickety bus where they sat crammed like sardines

in a can, one of the stubby iron rods another passenger held at the back seat poked mercilessly into Kitan's back. No form of adjustment remedied it. The smell of sweat and desperate humanity hung thick. The traffic outside was locked and loaded.

Beside him, T-Boss's laughter matched the conductor's bus-stop announcements and curses for hoarseness. Kitan turned his face to the window, fighting the urge to bash him with one of those rods. The whole spiritualist thing had been T-Boss' idea.

Ajebo, this your suffer no just fit you, rárá. I know somebody wey go fit help your matter.

"Vulture's beak and heart," he said in between sputters. "Three-day-old tortoise egg!"

Kitan pinched him to lower his voice and glanced around the heads that bobbed and swung as they dipped in and out of potholes. "Sand from my father's compound in the village," he added that technical impossibility in a wry whisper.

More laughter. "She must really like you o! Others don't get anything that straight-forward on the list."

"She said I can bring seventy-k instead, and she'll get the items I can't find for me," Kitan forced through a clogged throat. The sum dizzied him. His account hadn't crawled above fifteen thousand naira in months.

The laughter abated. T-Boss fixed his bulging eyes on him and leaned closer than the bus squashed them. "Nobody's head will go for it, not so?"

***

Yelling had become second nature. How else could you

prosper? Millions of people did it, just with different, more sophisticated mediums. For now, his voice was all he could afford.

It had vanished after the first week of the strange lifestyle, leaving him disgruntled with his chest and legs burning. It was how the guys in the area started to call him *Ajebo*. Now though, he could give orientations to others who were new to the business.

The mornings found him yelling, "Onigo Ode!" from street to street, buying plastic containers and used syringes from whoever had a stash to sell. It was hard that first time: returning to the plastic factory that had sacked him from his clerical work to sell the recycled materials. The afternoons found him yelling,

'Mile 2, Orile! Mile 2, Orile!', and whatever destinations the busses lined up by the road were headed until they filled up and left. The evenings found him yelling politics, football, and area matters in Yorùbá and Pidgin at *The Joint* with the other *alayes* – an army of unconventional entrepreneurs who were veterans in the yelling business – with Alomo Bitters clutched in his hand, the gin preparing to burn a trail down his throat.

This sweltering evening, the talk flowed well. The transformer had blown up again, so nobody knew when the area would have electricity. The Igbo guys down the street were really looking for *wahala*, and wahala they would get.

Remember Tunde with the big, big grammar and k-legs? He don go London o, imagine!

The vigilantes caught the person stealing people's chickens at night and beat him black and blue.

So as they don ban okada, make we throway our bike, abi? God punish them! Premier League go mad this year, o!

There was also talk about some sort of virus that had a funny name he forgot as soon as he heard it.

Baba Gesinde smacked him on the back of his head when he stared too long.

"*Ṣo wa pa?*" he yelled over the Fuji music blasting from the speakers, barring his yellowing teeth, the air thick with cigarette smoke and exhaustion. "You dey alright? You quiet today, o. Abi?" He glanced around their dozen odd groups for agreement. They obliged him. They had zeroed in on Kitan, fixed him their questioning stares. "No gist about Oga Ariyo?"

He was referring to Kitan's socialite boss, who lived in an Ikoyi duplex. It was his only job, twice weekly, that didn't involve yelling, just quiet nods, and relaying the area's political climate in polished English. He'd grabbed the opportunity, even if he would spend half the pay on transport back home. Ariyo was a strange man who had grown children all over the place that kept showing up, whom he kept introducing to his unsuspecting trophy wife as distant relatives. Waheed the gateman passed the gist of their commotion on to him. He passed it on to the guys.

Kitan shook his head. Nothing today. They muttered their disappointment. He gulped more Alomo.

Then he said, "Ejo, I go fit borrow money from

una?"

***

He awoke with a strangled yelp that was drowned out by the clap of thunder, drenched in sweat, trembling. In the dream – nightmare - he was back in the mansion with the voices, the poundings, the impassioned pleas, the senseless laughter, the resounding silence. He was poised over the WC, retching dry heaves. The usual hand was running unhurried strokes down his back. He had turned, ready to see her smiling, battered face, the face of the mistress turned wife, the face of his mother. He didn't.

It explained why his skin prickled and burned as the hand went. T-Boss' spiritualist stood, eyes glazed white, wizened claw suspended mid-air, mouth hanging so low it brushed the marble floor. "*Ajeeniruuun!*" came her curdling hiss.

A flash of lightning lit the room before plunging it back into pitch darkness. Outside, the crashing rain held the promise of a strenuous, flooded following day. He couldn't go back to sleep, so he lay there, steadying his racing heart, calculating, one arm plopped beneath his head, the other fending off the mosquitoes that made it past the netting and buzzed around little Grace, who stuck to him like glue, and Morayo, who released choppy snores.

Her rounded belly jutted into him, warm with life. She was all glorious curves and demure mannerisms those years ago when service to the broken and abused women at the SOS Foundation had thrust them together. These days, she was

32

angular and spitfire, her quiet strength mutating into fierce resolve. Those days, he couldn't wait to see her, to lose himself in her. These days, he just dreaded the sinking feeling of not having enough, of not *being* enough.

The fire she spat was hardly ever at him, though. She was his wife, his partner; he had her solidarity. It was the government that ran a system that would have an Accounting graduate like himself run odd jobs on the streets of Lagos, at the landlord of their Face-Me-I-Face-You one-room apartment with his garlic odour and drum stomach which only knows how to be collecting money when the house is falling apart; at that yeye Iya Sege who waited for me to start my fried yam business before starting her own just to frustrate me, but my God is still on the Throne; at the men whose mindless actions necessitated the creation of SOS.

These days, she stood at the window with her ingredient list and haggled prices with the passing hawkers until she checked them all off. If she had her way, she would storm the Iddo market and buy everything there.

KT, these road people will cut your throat if care is not taken!

But he couldn't stomach the thought of it, wouldn't risk her being jostled by the crowd. He would instead yell louder all day, every day.

Kitan couldn't breathe a word about the bizarre woman to Morayo. She would stare him down and ask if they were now begging on the streets if God was not alive.

He wasn't sure what his answer would be.

★★★

This time, Kitan heard the name of the virus properly, and it sank. Everyone concurred that it was too long, too fancy for something that promised darkness, and so, as the manner of mirth goes in Nigeria, it was dubbed *Coro*. News spread fast. The government announced a looming lockdown, during which everyone was meant to remain indoors 'until further notice,' which could mean anything.

At The Joint, the outrage was shared, opinions yelled, and humour inevitably conjured. Because in this life, you cannot frown forever. You just had to laugh at some point, or the grave would be much closer.

"*Irọ!* Fat lie! I no believe am. They just wan make life hard for people."

"How Oyinbo matter come take concern us, now? Why government go lock down everywhere? Abi na joke?"

"They say make we buy food keep for house."

"Ehh eh?" raised brows, incredulous smiles. "Them wan dash us the money, ni?"

"They say *Coro* dey kill plenty people for abroad o."

"Abeg o, *abeg!* I take God beg the people wey dey there. Make them stay put o. Make them no carry am reach this side. We no just want more wahala."

"*Joor!* If them like, make them come. *Coro* no

get levels where we dey. E no fit kill us." Everybody agreed with that one and cheered to it.

"Wo, that one no kuku concern me. Na my business I dey think." This was Kitan's view. Laughter and conversation pumped heartily for a while before they began to peter out.

Because slowly, the grim reality that faced them began to set in. Talk receded to whispered concerns, to slow and deliberate sipping from beer bottles, slow and deliberate contemplations. A lockdown meant many things: no chance to yell and hustle, no chance to gather, for anything at all. The guarantee of sustenance hung thin.

For Kitan, the list stretched a gut-wrenchingly further. Morayo said the baby was due in five weeks.

★★★

Grace had developed a tiny mole on her nose. She gave them solid, looped soundtracks of all the poems and rhymes she'd learnt at school. Her days involved drilling them with questions about everything, measuring her height against the wall, rubbing her small palms over Morayo's taut belly, and exclaiming when a kick came, pulling the skin of his face and giggling at his exaggerated reactions, regaling them with zigzagging stories about her classmates and teachers, shuffling about the room, replacing this with that, '*redocorating*', playing *Suwe* with the other compound children. She was the unwitting inventor of myriad, merciful distractions, and Kitan loved her all the more for it.

Her four-year-old chatter was incessant. *Daddy, I'm*

sooo happy you're home. You will carry me on your neck, ṣhebi? Mommy cannot play like that again o. My friend Tumishe said her mommy used to eat raw onions when she was pregnant (she would scrunch her nose and shudder) Thank God mommy doesn't do that. Daddy, you look tired, are you not resting well? Daddy, I'm hungry.

Time slowed to a maddening crawl. His insides in knots. The scanty palliatives of Indomie noodles sachets and twenty kilograms rice had been exhausted about a week ago, along with their savings and the money Baba Gesinde had lent him. Sneaking off to do whatever odd jobs presented themselves was getting increasingly difficult. Mama Ibinabo had given them as much credit sales as she could from her kiosk at the gate. They had accepted as much as shame would allow. Electricity had been thankfully restored, but it wouldn't be long before their bill expired, and they'd be back to square one.

From the thin wall separating their rooms, the voices of their neighbours, Akande and his wife Vero were grating, each hurled word a barb that made Kitan wince, that made cold sweat break out over him. The nightmare kept coming, and even though he knew how it would play out, he still awoke trembling. It was suddenly unthinkable, handing over even five thousand naira to the wizened spiritualist near Ikorodu, *Ajenirun* or no *Ajenirun.*

If he sat still any longer, he would implode.

***

The operation was swift, the way T-Boss envisaged it would be. The man was a loaded deputy to the Local Government Chairman. He lived in Lekki phase 1.

When the door swung open, delicious cool air rushed at them. T-Boss shoved the gun in the help's face before she could speak a word. He kept his colourless smile on as they ushered the family of five and their staff to the centre of parlour.

"I hope you're not too concerned that we aren't wearing masks?" T-Boss' brows actually furrowed. "If you like, we could move over to your bathroom and wash our hands." Multiple heads shook fervently, *no problem at all.*

"Well, won't you ask us to sit? Where are your manners?" he said, transferring his mock incredulous expression from householder to householder. The pot-bellied man sputtered the forced courtesy.

Kitan kept glancing back at the door, ears trained for sounds of trouble. His fingers trembled, kept squeezing and releasing the trigger of fake gun he held. His stomach gave a sickening pull. The other guys chuckled and sat. He followed suit. The lush leather couch felt like a caress.

"Your manners are bad o, *o ti bajẹ patapata,*" T-Boss shook his head, lips down-turned. "Won't you offer us food? Do I have to tell you people everything?" After which they produced amala with peppery, meat-riddled *Efọ Riro* soup, which the gang wolfed down in minutes. Kitan withdrew a nylon bag from his pocket and emptied his plate into it.

T-Boss had the man of the house heft a black polythene bag into the parlour. The crisp scent of currency circulated fast. T-Boss grinned. On their plasma TV, a blond CNN newscaster with a fancy British accent continued on about staggering death tolls and stimulus packages, about Work From Home and mental health.

"You people have jollof, for take-away?"

They did. They were equally generous with the surplus raw rice in their store. As they left, Kitan balanced the weight of his package under his arm. He would tell Morayo and the women at SOS it was palliative from Oga Ariyo.

★★★

Everything was going so well this third time. He used the back streets, the cover of dusk, and knowledge from his first two woeful attempts to make his way past the military checkpoints and the black Toyota Hiluxes that patrolled the area.

After fighting irrepressible concerns, growling stomachs, Morayo's crankiness - which he preferred to her silence - and cracking numerous dry jokes for days on end, he threw on a shirt and jeans and hit the road. He'd wasted too much time already. These spiritualists were all strange ways and biting repercussions. He couldn't deal with any of that, not on top of what he had on his plate.

His share of the Lekki loot was thirty thousand. There was no way on earth he would hand all of it over, just like that. He tried calling T-Boss to ask if she would accept 10k for now. He would know since he'd done business with her before, but the Glo operator kept repeating all sorts of things: *The number you're calling is busy, try later, goodbye; the number you're calling is out of cell coverage, please try again later; the number you're calling does not exist, please check the number and dial again.* Finally, there were no more words; just a single terminating beep.

So Kitan decided to chance it. One more day watching his family suffer would surely off him. He spent hours mapping out routes, anticipating dangers and ways out, evading Morayo's queries about what he was up to. Struggling not to implode.

"KT, KT," she paced as much as their cramped self-con would allow, shaking her head, supporting her waist, pulling on an earlobe. "Oluwakitan Joshua Adetade! How many times did I call you?" Grace kept glancing up from her position on the floor and the nightmare she was creating with crayons.

Morayo wagged a warning finger, voice tight with tears. They came too frequently these days.

"Whatever it is you're doing, stop it o! I'm telling you now. *Mi o ṣe wahala, o!* I smell trouble in this thing you're doing! Heh." She folded her slender arms over the great bulge of her belly. "Let nothing happen to you, o! Let nothing happen to you!"

She'd kept at the tirade until he was ready to leave. Kitan crushed her to himself as much as her belly would allow, pressed a kiss to her lips.

"*Mo,*" her name bubbled from a depth he didn't know existed, barely audible. His eyes burned, but not as fiercely as the sinking premonition in his chest. Morayo buried her face against his pounding heart for what felt like an eternity. It was one of those moments when their thoughts melded in that way he still did not understand. In her embrace, there was fear, pain and acceptance.

When he finally moved, she clutched the base of his shirt in her fist, voice now placating, like how she spoke when Grace was sick or upset "*Oya*, at least eat something. *Ejor*, please."

He'd swallowed a few balls of *eba* and *ewedu* soup to please her.

Now, he wished he didn't. Because, at the vicious bark and a loud, "Hey you!" The food raced up his throat and began a painful squirm for freedom.

The stocky SARS officer with the panting Rottweiler reached him at the intersection. The small market beside them sat eerily silent as darkness fell. "Who you be? Where you dey go?" he yelled for backup and jabbed a finger in Kitan's face.

"You just land for here? You no know say lockdown dey?"

Kitan tried to get the planned excuse out. It wasn't working. "*Soro soke, werey*! Will you open that your dirty mouth and speak louder?"

His four companions gathered round.

Kitan's heart pounded.

The leader's bloodshot eyes narrowed. "*Kini*? You dumb?"

Kitan shook his head no. He tried again. "I-I just

w-w-wanted to reach t-the ph-pharmacy.”

“Pharmacy? Who sick? Na you? You get Coro?”

“No, no, it’s—”

“Baba, this guy dey give you lie chop! See as him leg dey shake like fish, now!” shouted another one.

They sized him up.

“Wetin dey the bag?”

Kitan’s heart sank.

“Na money? Because I no trust the way wey you take dey hold am tight like say na your life, *rárá*. You thief am? Na operation you just dey return from?”

Kitan gulped and shook his head.

“Baba, e too dey obvious! This guy resemble thief, now! Look am wella,” It was the same muscled instigator from before. “I sure say him dey do *G,* join. Trace am now, you go find laptop everywhere wey he dey use dupe people. No mind him baby face, o." Then to him, “*Oya*, submit that bag for search.”

In an instant of terror-induced irrationality, Kitan turned and ran. It was the shortest chase ever. They pulled him to the ground.

“Baba, I tell you say this guy na scam. *You dey run? Run go where, now? Imagine this guy, o! Imagine this guy!”

He started to beg. Wetness seeped into his shirt; he’d crashed into a muddy, refuse-lined puddle.

The first punch came. Then another. And then another.

★★★

In this new version of the dream, several fingers trailed

down his back, ragged, biting. Turning, he found the man with the scar beside the spiritualist; the man with the cool gaze, with the moustache. The man Maami had remained fastened to until he offed her. His father's hand hovered in the air, then fell.

Kitan jerked awake, hit a bare body, earned himself curses and a sharp shove that sent waves of pain sliding down to his fingertips.

It had been worse that first day.

Other heads showed in the sickly yellow light of the single bulb that hung from the ceiling. The air was putrid with old sweat, rot, and forlorn humanity. Brushing bodies, coarse conversation, and sour unbelievable stories – it exceeded all the prison cell stereotypes he'd ever known. His meal for the past week had been half-cooked beans sprinkled with white garri. It was quite the update to his exciting CV.

His new friend Paluzo knew something about all sixteen inmates: who was really guilty and who was not, whose festering injury contributed to the stench, who was there permanently and who was due to be let out soon. The oddly plump, grey-haired man told him that he was on that last category: "Them need space to put more offenders. Your issue no bad like that."

The certainty of never seeing a person again that pushes one to loosen shields and pour out their soul pushed Kitan, and he left nothing out. Paluzo listened with the grim raptness of a psychologist and responded with a plethora of biting questions.

Wetin he do na terrible thing, but why not forgive your papa and free your mind? This T-Boss guy wey carry you go meet the juju woman, him life better? He don establish? You think sey the 70k na once and for all? You think say she go stop at money? You get pikin, abi? What if she ask for your Grace? You never even reach 30 years, abi? All this energy you dey burn for this matter, why not burn am for one single hustle wey you get passion for?

★★★

He wept with Morayo after the trailer driver that gave him a free ride dropped him off. Grace cried too, clutching him harder than her mother.

There was another cry that stopped him cold: shrill, livid at having her attention shared with this strange, battered man. Kitan cradled her tiny body and wept more. The neighbours knocked to say *Modupe, Oluwa, thank God o!* Pastor Kayode laid hands on him and spoke in tongues.

After the lengthy confession, a tight-lipped Morayo set the stage for a DIY treatment session that had the old wounds throbbing afresh. Then she forced a tangy herbal mix down his throat.

Kitan drifted in and out of a weightless, dreamless sleep.

★★★

"That spiritualist? She don die o."

It sounded like a piece of information the diminutive man in greasy blue overalls thoroughly enjoyed sharing. After weeks of tentative easing, the lockdown was finally lifted. Several people stepped in with help and, miracle of miracles, they had gotten by.

"She don *kpeme*," the man repeated. "They say na Coro." He leaned closer to Kitan, who had blood roaring in his ears, and lowered his voice, matter-of-factly, "Me, I say na her juju chop her. She overdo. Very evil person."

Then he straightened and eyed Kitan.

"I hope say you no give am any money, sha?"

★★★

He sat on the stairs of the neatly plastered Pentecostal Church on the way home, drew in crisp air and completed his SOS.

It had begun that very day when an unfounded love had pulled him and Maami to Chief's mansion, deepened with the vicious abuse, grew in length over the long years of running, of trying to forget.

Somewhere within those quiet hours, as self-centredness cracked under the weight of sober reflection, he remembered countless others who were fighting all sorts of battles: the afraid; the hungry for food, for peace, for love; the broken by circumstance, by others, by pandemic, by themselves. Then there were the ones who weren't even aware they were broken.

Save Our Souls! From Mankind, With Much Heaviness.

God must really get truckloads of them per second, rendered both consciously and otherwise. Anyhow, he added his to the catalogue. Didn't people say He heard

45

and did radical things about their conditions? What did he have to lose by trying? That was that. He had come, he had delivered the message.

He was a leaf when he left at sundown, light enough for the wind to carry him.

★★★

A gleaming black Mercedes stood in front of the compound. The man who leaned against it was speaking with Morayo, who was gesturing animatedly. She caught his confused gaze and stilled.

The man turned.

Kitan froze.

The man with the scar, with the cool gaze, with the moustache. The one who authored Maami's fate, the nightmares, the running, the heaviness.

The man had tears swimming in his eyes.

Aninoritse Ejuliuwa is a lover of inspiring words, whether in a book or a song. She believes that impactful storytelling bears the capacity for positive transformation, and is one of the most potent tools for sharing the Creator's Love in a world in desperate need of healing.

She is currently a Development Economics Masters student at Georg-August University, Göttingen, Germany. Aninoritse is passionate about contributing to a society where people possess the freedom and empowerment to excel in their unique paths. Behind the scenes, she is working on her debut novel.

CHILDREN OF CHUKWU

♥

Amara Ozokwelu

I walk around the compound, over the carpet formed by the fallen leaves of the mango tree, through the spread of the Ugwu leaves Nne had planted, till I see the black earth dotted by flowers aesthetically grown around the ground where Papa was lain eight years ago.

"I am now a warrior, Papa," I mutter under my breath, careful lest anyone see me speaking to the air.

"I can now fight for you," I whisper, my hands gripping the dagger blessed by the gods at the celebration to kill all of my enemies.

The initiation of warriors had gone the way I had imagined, the aggressive dancing of the warriors punctuated with gunshots, their strong legs raising dusts as they threw their weights on the ground. The crowd of older men and women pressed together, watching the procession with awe, while the children tried to mimic the intricate dance steps, throwing their legs and shaking their shoulders to the beat of the drums.

My heart swelled with pride when I was called one of the new warriors, proud to be one of the bare-chested teenage boys becoming men with skin stretched taut over muscles, rippling with strength, and impassive faces to show bravery and maturity.

The men of Nanka village were known for their heroics and tall, formidable statures and incredible fighting skills.

There was a proverb that said it was easier to throw a mountain to the ground than a Nanka warrior's back to touch the red ground, so I stood extra tall, stretching my back to make up for my shorter legs and feminine features that had almost made me unworthy of being a warrior.

I inflated my chest, raised my brows, and pinched my lips, my eyes darting through the crowds, taking in the combined look of shock from most men and women and admiration from the young girls at seeing me, a woman, become a warrior.

Everyone that stood around me towered over me but I reminded myself how I had bested most of them in the rigorous training and games that qualified me as the first female Nanka warrior, so I made fists with my hands pushing all my fears and insecurity in the dark room, deep in the corner of my brain where I kept memories of the night, I watched papa hacked to death.

Agummadu, the leader, had stood in front of the new warriors, his black blade reflecting the sun each time he moved, flexing his hefty shoulders as he riled the crowds to a frenzy while he recited the slogan of the warriors

"Nanka Warriors!" Agummadu shouted.

"No mercy!" I replied, my high-pitched voice drowned by their baritones, but that did not stop me from shouting louder.

"Nanka warrioooorrrssss!"

"Kill all our enemiessss!" I screamed to match his tempo.

Agummadu had drawn six long cuts on my chest with his black blade and as I bled, the village priest had said prayers mopping my blood with a white cloth. The cuts that will turn to scars were proof that I had brought honour to my father's name and that one day, I would defeat my enemies and bring destruction and pain to the land of Ago.

I whisper again: "I can now fight for you Papa." before I return to the house, my head bowed with the weight of all the things that could have been.

★★★

Ago was a village without culture where there were no gods, a 'cursed place' Papa had called it countless times, shaking his head while rolling his shoulders and snapping his fingers as he told tales of their abominable acts; how the men in their village left the farm activities to the women while they laid on raffia mats doing nothing.

I wondered what Papa would think of me if he were alive, a woman warrior fighting with a blade. I wondered if he would have called it an abomination, like half the elders had called it, throwing spittle on the floor when I had volunteered for the training.

My father had called the abomination of Ago men an affront to the gods. "Chukwu had not created man to lazily lie in wait for their women to tend to them," papa had said, and this explained why the village was cursed, why the sky rarely blessed their lands with water.

The enmity between my village and Ago had existed for many years, even before my grandfather was born. My father had told me it all started when the King of Ago and his son visited the king of Nanka, my village, to ask for his only daughter's hand in marriage to foster the unity between the two villages.

The celebration of their marriage had gone on for days and the then king of Nanka, my king had gifted the new couple the most fertile plot of land that stood beside the river. It was considered a gesture that showed the bond the two villages now shared. An Igbo man never gave out his land, lands were prized possessions as the grounds tied you to your ancestors and should always be guarded from outsiders.

All was well until the new husband of the King's daughter sent her back to her father's house with tales of her promiscuity. She had called the name of another man while the prince was inside of her, their bodies singing old tunes of procreation. She was labelled *akwuna* – a lustful woman that seeks the pleasures of other men.

The marriage was over; a prince could never marry a lady whose body yearned for another man and whose body had a dangling tool between his legs.

A bride sent back to her father's home was a shame that burnt the ears and caused men to hide, shunning Umunna meetings till the news blew over, but to send home a king's daughter was an insult to the entire community. The community bristled with anger, even toddlers that filled their mouths with sand were inactive, as the entire community mourned their shame.

The tension multiplied after the suicide of the King's daughter and the entire community screamed for vengeance resulted in a war that attributed to the loss of lives from both villages.

The two villages had burnt and bled till the royals agreed on a truce and the return of the gifted land as a sign of peace.

Many years have passed, and the gifted land was still the cause of chaos and bloodshed. Ago village, in a severe season of drought, had claimed the land as rightfully theirs, and the killings and unrest had continued, taking my father along with it.

I was consumed with the need to prove myself, to pay back in grief the debt I owed to the scared faces of Ago warriors.

★★★

"Those men should not be allowed to come into our village, talk more of dining with us when our women and children are present," Agummadu spat, reiterating his view on his displeasure of the oath cleansing ritual *iko mmee.*

"*Tufiakwa*! They want to dis-virgin and disgrace more of our women, *o kwa ya.* The king is too blind to see this," he continued as he mopped the beads of sweat on his face that was the colour of red dust glowering at the armed men of Ago village standing at the far side of the field.

I and the rest of the warriors have been assigned to ensure the peace of the oath cleansing ritual. The blood-soaked soil of our villages would be cleansed by the scooping away of the blood-sodden earth by the chief priests of both communities.

The ritual was done to usher in a new era of peace and puts a seal of agreement between the villages and their gods.

I watched the procession, observing the uneasiness of the kings at sharing a table with a lifelong enemy. A massive celebration would begin once the priests were done pouring libations on the ground and sacrificing the many livestock provided for the ritual.

The two priests worked in unison, their bald heads, red coverings, and dark tattoos were the only thing they had in common for my priest was as tall as a palm tree, rolling his head and hunched shoulders with every incantation that poured freely out of his lips while the priest of Ago was small and round his pot stomach an unusual attribute of those chosen by gods.

The peace ritual changed nothing about how I felt; my blade hungered for the blood of Ago men.

There was no scooping of Papa's blood and no burying of hatchets till the thing inside me that grew every day, feeding on my life force, sucking away all of my joy sank its teeth into the blood of Ago warriors and carved its name in history.

Time moved like a snail, each step of the ritual dragging on for longer than I expected until I noticed him, my eyes locking with his. Most men shot daggers at me with their eyes or shamelessly leered at me, but his look was different. His eyes spoke lengthy words of awe and desire, and I did not want to look away.

The two long scars on both sides of his face made most Ago men resemble *ekwensu,* but it suited him perfectly. The dark scars, a colourful contrast to his skin, a rich yellow, the colour of overripe pawpaw and his long legs like the trunk of a coconut tree made me give him the name Anyanwu, the god of the sun.

I watched him walk towards me, and I found myself walking to meet him halfway, my steps light with new purpose, the innate desire to know this man that bored holes into my mind till I am standing before him, the ritual forgotten; parallel would never meet.

"You are not allowed to look at me that way," I say,

meeting his gaze, the blade in my hand unnaturally heavier.

"I thought we were here to broker peace," he replied, his full lips stretching into a toothless smile.

I clenched my jaws.

"In my village, women with front teeth that never meet are almost worshipped," he said, his face impassive. "It is considered the ultimate form of beauty for the gods to bless your teeth."

His voice was exactly like I thought it would be, it felt like drinking cold water gotten from a calabash on a sunny day. I search for words to say to avoid sounding like a young maiden meeting a man for the first time.

"I would like to know who cut you," he said, frowning at my chest

"Why?" I reply, my grip on my blade loosening. I had never felt so free with anyone, including my kin, and it bothered me this connection that felt like it had been formed in my past life.

"I would like to cut him to pieces for daring to draw lines on a skin this flawless, cocoa smeared with oil."

I tried hard to hide the smile on my face and the heartbeat that screamed in my ears.

"You do realize you're threatening my leader at a peace ritual, and this could cost you your head."

He looked away from me and watched the crowd "If this goes well, this war can finally be over."

"The ritual cannot bring the dead to life," I say, staring at him. I reminded myself he was still the enemy. "It cannot bring food to the widows and orphans; your men have made."

"We have all lost someone in this war, Agu,"he said solemnly, looking right into my eyes.

"Agu?" I ask.

"Well, I hear you fight like a lion," he replied with a small laugh that softened his features. I wished he would laugh more so I could see his full nose wrinkle again and his eyes disappear into their sockets.

I don't feel the need to defend myself, to let the thing inside my body embrace me like it did whenever I interacted with men, where every sentence was layered with mockery.

I sense his respect, evident in how he folded his hands behind him, so I smile, pushing the thing far into the corners of my mind. I feel the need to peel off the layers of covering and relax into the strange need of my body to be seen by him and to appreciate his god-like features. The loud noise from the ritual felt like it was miles away; it was just him and I standing under the full glare of the sun.

"Peace is a fragile thing," I say. "It is hard to lose people but even harder when their chi has not called them, and their life is brutally stolen from their body."

"We are all scared and bearing the weight of our

pain, some more than others," he mumbled softly, pain etched in his face as he willed his eyes to meet mine while I stared into the crowd.

"What we choose to do with the pain is what matters," he continued. "I am sorry about the death of your father."

I wonder how he knows about papa, and I remember how the entire village had talked about his death, so I fight the urge to weep and rid myself of all the tears I never let free. I want him to stop talking about papa as I am too tired to retreat into my shell, so I let him speak as I feel the first drop of tears fall from my eyes.

"I am sorry you had to watch him die," he said, his hands reaching for my palm.

I hear gunshots, the hastened movements of feet, the cry of a child, and the scream of a warrior in pain and know the ritual was over and chaos still lived in my land but I continue to lock eyes with him till he hits his blade with my blade; a sign of peace and understanding since the days of my ancestors, a sad smile on his face as he says" I guess, we can never be free."

I watch him disappear into the crowd, his blade clashing with the blade of my kin, as I swiftly draw the blood of a young Ago warrior, slicing open his stomach, and I know, I would never know the name of the man that looked like Anyanwu and made me feel whole. He, like me, was a child of Chukwu born into a world of hate.

Amara Ozokwelu was born in Lagos, Nigeria. Growing up, she found joy in reading as many books as she could find. She has a bachelor's degree in Microbiology and currently works as a quality control analyst at an FMCG company in Lagos, Nigeria. She enjoys writing fiction, reading books, watching movies, and having fun conversations.

LOVE AFTER DEATH

♥

Chikaira E-Edonkumoh

My husband is coming home tonight.

I've waited for him all day, and when the short hand on the clock hits twelve, he'll sit right beside me. We'll talk for hours. He always has something interesting to say and has a way of leaving me with a thought to ponder on but has since stopped making love to me. When I need to feel his touch, he'll lay by me and wrap his arms around me. I always wonder what he gets up to during the times he's not with me, whenever I ask him, his jaw tightens and there's something in his eyes which are usually so guileless, even when he says everything is fine.

My mother doesn't like him, and she makes no secret of it even after ten years of marriage. Our first discussion was while I was in my last quarter of national youth service duty. She made an impromptu visit when I didn't visit her for three straight weekends. It was a duty I abhorred.

"I don't trust that Jide boy, with his charming looks," she says, tapping the ladle at the edge of the pot on the stove. She swipes the ladle on her palm and licks her palm before nodded her approval then gestures at me. As I hand her the bowl of freshly cut pumpkin leaves, I chew on the inside of my cheek, waiting for more berating. She empties it into the pot without stirring it in. She turned around slowly to face me, hugging herself.

"Will he stay? Even if he wanted to, will these Lagos girls let him?"

All through her rants and tantrums, I say nothing; I didn't need to because Jide always proved her and her baseless suspicions wrong.

Now twenty years and counting, I sit on the bed and look up at the clock placed intently above the door.

It's exactly 12 a.m. This will be our tenth wedding anniversary without a candlelight dinner. Everyone has forgotten except Henry, our first son, because it is also his birthday. I didn't believe I would join the queue of women desperate to have a child for their husband. And that I did four years. I had given up. My monthly cycle didn't desist it's confronting me with my predicament. So I didn't consider going to the doctor until my stomach was swollen. I was so shocked that I was almost five months gone that I actually drank a full bottle of Smirnoff.

I almost scream as I feel Jide's ice-cold hands on my thigh bring me back to the present. After all this time, he's still looked the same, not even a beard or moustache. The same short curly hair in varied colours of brown, the same hooked nose, dark pink, plump lips, honey-brown eyes that turns golden in the sunlight. He's so perfect, it's almost surreal, like a fluid dream. In that instant, I understand why my mother is so sceptical. I run my fingers through his hair and he pulls me in for a kiss, which he never lets linger.

"Hey beautiful," he said, looking at me intently with his smiling eyes as he strokes my cheek.

"How was work?" I ask just to say something as I try to steady my frazzled nerve.

"Let's not talk about work. I have a better idea."

I look at him expectantly because I didn't see a parcel in his hands; neither was he hiding them behind him. He steps out for a minute and comes in with some DVD's and two spoons. I give him a puzzled look before his *idea* sinks in.

"We are taking a trip down memory lane." It comes out as a statement rather than a question.

I shrug.

While he puts on our wedding DVDs, I take out a tub of ice-cream from the mini-fridge next to my side of the bed. Minutes later, I'm in his arms, ice-cream in hand laughing at the TV screen. I'm freezing; his arms are comfortable but so so cold - almost as cold as the plate in my hand. But I feel like the luckiest woman in the world, and I sleep with a content smile on my face.

I wake up knowing. Knowing my husband is not by my side and immediately wish I was still asleep. He didn't even stay for breakfast. I grudgingly tear myself off the bed and make my way to the kitchen to find my mother hovering. I'm now used to it. I let her as she had no one to bother but me, the curse of being an only child.

"Mummy, good morning," I call out from over my shoulder; she already made breakfast and served some for me.

"Mummy, you didn't have to, I've told you. You're a guest here -"

"Ehn?! Guest where? In my daughter's house, *Biko*. Stop that joke." She flapped the kitchen towel a few times before replacing it by the oven.

I smile and take a bite of the food, boiled yam and eggs fried with beef and vegetables. I didn't realise how hungry I was until then. I bit my lower lip when I saw her wiping her dry hands on the apron repeatedly and knew a lecture was about to start. She hadn't changed. She would sigh a few times, then clear her throat noisily as she pulls out a chair and smooths her hand over her wrapper...

"Ego." my mother called solemnly.

"Yes," I mumble from a stuffed mouth deliberately chewing slowly so food would be in my mouth.

"Ego," she says slowly for dramatic effect.

One look at her serious face and I drop the fork and take a gulp of water.

"Mum, what is it?" I ask while recalling the last time I saw this look on her face.

I remember with startling clarity that it was ten years ago; I came home from the doctor's with the news. I was pregnant! Henry was five years old at the time. Before I could say anything, she sat me down, and with this same look, she told me Jide had died in a car accident at the Benin-Ore road on his way home. There were no survivors.

"Wait, what? But I'm pregnant." At that revelation, she broke down and started crying. My mum, crying, blubbering, like a little girl in my arms. This had to be a dream. A terrible sick twisted nightmare that played on for months. I pinched myself, but - it went on. I slapped myself - it went on. Perhaps if I slit my wrists - it still wouldn't end. The same faces at our wedding were now at my husband's funeral barely six month's later.

My unborn baby might have sensed the grief and opted out. I had a miscarriage, and that was the straw that broke the camel's back. I went to the backyard to the heap of red mud they said they kept my husband in. I came with a planned speech, a declaration of my love for him; if I had done anything, he should forgive me and come back so things could be okay. Let everything go back to the way it was. But as always, I lost focus and broke down on his grave. I continued everyday, then weeks and months. My tears and saliva and sweat fell on the red soil. The moist soil clung to my clothes, in-between my toes, and socked the sole of my feet.

I would go and visit Jide in his new house. We would talk as usual. The only difference was that he was under the pile of dust, and his voice was in my head. Mother saw everything but said nothing. To her, that was my way of coping; her way was burying her head in her bible and hanging crosses and rosaries on every doorway in the house. As soon as his death was a year old, my mother got my cousins to bundle me back to the city. It was time to move on. But I sneaked out late at night and travelled back to my husband's side.

My nightmare was now my reality, I thought to myself as I headed to Jide's grave for an evening session. There was a huge load of guilt that lay on my shoulders that day. Maybe I let him die? That Friday night; before he left, He stood by the door of our bedroom, briefcase in hand. With a torn look on his face as if leaving me would literally kill him. "Are you sure you'll be fine? It'll be just you and mama in the house," he had repeated.

"Yes, I'll be fine," I snapped already beginning to feel smothered

"Are you sure you'll cope without me?" he asked.

I sigh dramatically. "Yes, baby, I'll be fine. Now get going before you miss your flight," I said, shoving him out the door. He held me in place and looked deep into my eyes like he could see right through me. I looked away. I felt naked and vulnerable under his gaze, but he brought his lips to mine. The kiss ended with an audible smack and left me dizzy.

"I really, really don't want to go," he said before he left. He left with hunched shoulders. I frown. I have only just remembered noticing that.

★★★

"Ego! Ahn ahn are you not going to answer my question?!"

I blinked. "Sorry, mum, you were saying?"

She lets out a deep breath and looks at me through squinted eyes, searching for something then inhaled deeply. "I heard voices in your room last night."

"Voices?" I ask absent-mindedly. My thoughts were back on the day Jide died. He didn't carry his boarding pass; it was on the bureau with the car keys on it.

"Yes, giggling and laughing."

I snicker humourlessly.

She drags her chair closer. "Ego, you are my only child. So you have all my attention. You know you can tell me anything."

"Oh, for goodness sake!" I rise, but her hand rests on my arm firmly, and I sit down.

"Why are you exposing me to the wind?" she asks and pulls at the edge of her wrapper and makes an event of blowing her nose, and then she sniffs a few times. "You've become a mirror of yourself. Talking to yourself in your sleep was manageable. But talking to yourself loudly and giggling too,

66

tufiakwa!"

I raise an eyebrow. *How does she come up with these things?*

"What is wrong with talking and giggling?"

"Nothing, if you are watching a movie. Nothing, if it is with friends, but to yourself?"

I let out a long desperate sigh.

"Ego, madness does not run in this family. Please, let it not start with you."

"What!?"

"Talking to yourself is not normal *su'nwôm*," my mother pleaded with tears in her eyes.

"You think I've been talking to myself?"

"But of course, who else is in this house but you and I?"

"How about my husband?"

My mother removes the headtie that shielded her greying hair. She scratches her head vigorously. It was a gesture that shows she had reached her limit. I'm hoping she has because this invasion of hers is becoming unnerving. Her legs are shaking as she hugs herself and shudders. It's fascinating that she is able to do all of that and still mutter. I continue to look at her though.

★★★

A while past.

"Anyway, when are you going to start dating?"

"Mummy! Not again. Is that why you made me breakfast? Ehn? So you can cajole me into cheating on my husband?"

"Ego, my dear child… Jide is dead!"

"Stop it! Stop It! Stop telling lies. I know you don't like him… you've never liked him. So just stop!"

"Ego, I worry about you. It's over ten years now. You have to move on. Let him go. Please."

She waits for an answer, and even though she gives me all the time in the world, I say nothing. I know she's right; I know Jide is gone, but I can't let him go. I won't let him go. I spent all my life searching for Mr. Perfect, and here he is, just not the way I planned.

Chikaira E-Edonkumoh is a Nigerian short story writer, poet, and influencer.

NOTES ON LOVE

Testimony Odey

To love is to suffer.

Those were the words your mother told you when you first asked why my father threw her across the wall in a maddening rage. You were thirteen then and it wasn't the first time you saw your father hit your mother, but you had never had the guts to ask why he did what he did. Ever since you had the ability to understand what went on around you, you knew your father was an abusive partner.

In the earliest of your memories, you remember him asking why the house was always unclean. Your mother looked at him, sighed and rolled her eyes. He screamed something like, "How dare you? Am I your mate?" And when he got no reaction, the punching began. Mother had her hands over her head, trying to protect herself and he only stopped when she was on the floor, screaming and rocking herself like a baby.

Only years later did you understand why Mother ignored Father when he complained about the uncleanness of the house. You lived in a majestic duplex with five rooms and six toilets and Mother had to cook, clean the house, weed the garden, wet the plants, wash the toilets and it was impossible to do it all. In the earliest of your memory, you remember that your father was an insensitive person.

You are the only child and your childhood is nothing to speak of and when you hear people saying that one's childhood is golden, you wonder how. You would wake in the morning, prepare for school, take the school bus, attend classes and go back home. You never really went out, except to school, church, and family members' houses.

You were always the odd one out, skin so dark that someone once said nobody would see you in the night.

When you turned thirteen, you had hope that life would get better, that you would go out often (or sneak out of the house, if need be), that you would engage yourself in so many after-school activities that you wouldn't have to spend much time home. You attend classes because you must; teachers are not the nicest to you, considering that you're not really a bright student. Students are not the nicest either, as they are always making fun of your poor marks in tests. You don't really concentrate at school because all you're thinking about is why your parents are always at loggerheads.

You're turning fifteen very soon and you're not very excited about your birthday. There's nothing to be excited about – your birthday is a reminder that you're getting older and you haven't achieved as much as you should. When you were thirteen, you made a list of things you wanted to achieve before you turned eighteen.

The list included writing a book (you didn't care about publishing, all you wanted to know was that there was a mind-blowing full-manuscript written by you), writing a letter to both your parents (you would love to ask them why they got married in the first place if all they did was scream and hit each other), registering in a book club, learning the piano and singing. There were too many obstacles to your goals, for example, your parents thought writing fiction was stupid.

Father caught you writing a couple of times and did not hesitate to tear it to pieces, telling you that you could use that time studying.

Mother was less harsh, if she caught you writing, she'd read a few sentences, compliment your work and ask what you plan to do with it. You would say nothing and then she would say that if you had no plans for whatever you were writing, you should be studying instead.

Now, for the book club, you needed the permission of your parents to join, and you already knew that they would not grant it to you. You had prayed about everything, had shown God the list of your endless goals and asked Him to help you achieve even one, had asked Him to make life easier for you and had asked Him if to love was to truly suffer. You knew he had heard your cry when your school announced the opening of a new club – the instruments club – where you could learn any instrument of your choice. There were different rooms for different instruments, so the melodies erupting from one instrument do not clash with another.

You're the only student who has signed up for piano lessons because most of the students are not really interested in music or prefer to play instruments like the violin, guitar, flute and harp. It is only when playing the piano that you manage to forget most of your life troubles. You're a quick learner and your fingers tap on the piano keys so delicately and beautifully that Mr. Raymond, the piano teacher thinks you're extremely talented.

"You are passionate when you play the piano and I think that passion could be a major source of motivation," he once said. When you got home that day, you wrote in your diary:

I am passionate about the piano.
Mr. Raymond said so.
He's a really nice teacher; he's forever saying kind things to
me.
I look forward to going to piano class every break time.
I would rather not eat so I could spend more time with the
piano and Mr. Raymond. they make me really happy.

Your school is a disciplined school, and you always have to have your socks white, hair plaited according to the hairstyle and uniforms ironed so you would not get into trouble. Once every term, there is a day called 'career day.' Before this day, a list will be passed on asking every student what they wanted to become when they grew up.

Then on career day, you would dress up as your future profession and before everyone in the hall, you'd state what inspired you, how your career could help humanity and then pledge to study hard so you could become what you wanted to be. It was not compulsory though as there were students who didn't care to fill the list, but majority of the students chose to do so, resulting in major presentations throughout the day and therefore, no classes at all. You did not fill your space in the career day sheet, not because you didn't care about your future but because you had no idea what you wanted to be. You were so confused – life was really mean sometimes.

Tomorrow is career day, but you are wearing your uniform as normal, not a special cloth that would attract statements like, 'You'd make a pretty beautiful doctor.' 'You'd make a handsome basketball player.' You do not plan to go to the hall, where the presentations will be ongoing. You plan to spend every inch of your minute in the instrument room, playing the piano and listening to Mr. Raymond's voice.

You iron your skirt which is a little bit above your knees and the white shirt. Then you try to sleep and when you finally feel sleepy, your parent's screams wake you up. Grumpily, you walk to the living room where they seem to have created a World War three.

"I have lived with your trash for long enough! If not for Ada, I would be long gone!" Mother screamed.

"Go! You should take your things and get out of my house!" Father retorted.

"Point of correction, this is our house. We saved to buy this land where this house stands on!"

"I contributed majority."

"It doesn't matter. My contribution is part of what now puts a roof over our heads. I don't even know why I married you."

"You're not the same person I knew."

"You're also not the same person I knew."

"I hate this marriage," Father whispered and walked out. You wondered why he did not resort to beating Mother as was the usual practice whenever they quarrelled. When you go back to your room, you write in your diary:

My parents hate the fact that they are married.
Father said Mother wasn't the same person he had married.
Mother said so too.
The only thing constant in life is change.
I thought this marriage thing was supposed to be for better, for worse. As circumstances change, for better, for worse, people change too…but that doesn't mean you should stop loving them. At least that's what I think.
Mother was right when she said, 'to love is to suffer', because when you love someone, you put up with all their flaws and shit and even when you scream and say hurtful words

at them, it's because you're hurt at that moment, not because you've stopped loving them.

Love is a wicked thing and I know this because every time father hits mother and she gets better, she likes to pretend it never happened and it's almost like she's saying: you can break and hurt my heart, but when it heals, it beats for you.

It makes me mad.

I once told Mother that I felt like boiling hot water and pouring it on Father for all the pain he had ever taken her through, and she hushed me.

She said, "you'd hurt him badly if you did that."

And I'm like, "He's been hurting you badly for so long and all those terrible memories of him punching you and making you cry are forever etched in my brain. they won't go away. I can't forget and pretend it never happened like you always do afterwards."

And she said: "He'll change. He's working on himself, on becoming a better husband. He's not always like that, abusive and stupid; he's really nice sometimes too. He's happy and lovely and romantic and a good husband. He's all that too. We all have our bad sides…and we are all working to be better people. He'll change."

That was when I decided that love was a dangerous thing.

To love is truly to suffer.

You want to write more but the ink in your pen finishes and you sigh.

The next day, you practice your smile in front of the mirror, while repeating positive affirmations. It's early in the morning and school is filled with so many future doctors, football players, cooks, teachers, dancers and when anyone asks what you want to be, you smile and say nothing. The piano room is locked and you sit on the floor in front of the room, your legs criss-crossed, waiting for Mr. Raymond. The other instrument rooms are locked and you have your chin resting on your palms while your small bag and diary lies beside you. You did not bother to bring any of your exercise books, considering that there would be no class today. While waiting, you write in your diary:

Twelve dancing princesses
Each wearing glass slippers
Looking for their Prince Charming
Hoping to be wrapped around in the arm
Of a knight ever so strong and mighty.
Twelve dancing princesses
Twirling under the full moon
Ears searching for the voice of
Their Prince Charming
Hoping to hear sweet words from
A knight ever so strong and mighty.
Twelve dancing princesses
Sitting under the oak trees
The night is long gone
And the sun rises up with a sparkling glow.
They've waited all night
For their Prince Charming
But he doesn't seem to be coming any time soon
And they are getting tired of
Waiting and waiting for
A knight ever so strong and mighty.

I'm waiting for Mr. Raymond. he has the key to the piano room. he's probably going to be shocked that I'm not in the hall doing any presentations whatsoever. I've really been thinking of writing a book but I'm not sure. I'm not sure if I'm a good enough writer. I'm not sure if people will like what I write.

"Ada?" A voice calls.

You lift your head up and your heart takes a leap. "Good morning, Mr. Raymond."

"How are you?" he smiles, putting his hand in his bag, searching for the key of the Piano Room. He's standing right in front of you, and you close your diary and move out of the way. He unlocks the door, and you hang your small bag over your shoulder and enter the room.

"I'm good," you say and smile. The room is dim-lighted and so, you begin to open the windows.

"You're not participating in Career Day?" Mr. Raymond asks as he places his bag on the table. The room is clean and dustless, because it is cleaned by the cleaners every afternoon before school shuts down.

"Well, I don't know what I want to be yet. And I'd rather play the piano instead of being in a hall filled with noise."

He stops in his tracks and looks at you strangely. "You don't know what you want to be?" he asks again for clarity and you sigh.

"Let's just say I haven't discovered myself," You say.

He draws out seats for you both.

"What do you like doing?" he asks.

"I love to write but I'm afraid people won't like what I write. My parents don't even like to see me write." There was something about Mr. Raymond that made you so free with him, that made you feel safe, that made your tongue fast to divulge your greatest thoughts, that made it easy for you to pour out your heart and soul with the confidence that he would not take advantage of you.

"It's like they don't want to see me happy, especially my dad. He comes in and my mom and I start shaking because he's got these insane anger issues and slams his fists on the table when talking. It's like he's trying to make everyone afraid of him and I really hate it. I can't wait to make my own money and bullshit him.

He's so insensitive, always hitting my mom and screaming at her and throwing insults at me whenever he's got the chance. I don't even know why my mom is still with him. To love is to suffer. I hate this life."

You are breathless by the time you've stopped talking and you slam your palms over your mouth because you are sure you've said too much. However, you feel like a heavy weight has been lifted off your chest. Mr. Raymond looks a little bit thoughtful, like he's trying to digest everything you've just told him. He runs his fingers over his hair and takes a deep breath.

"I think you would make a good writer and I

think people will like your work. You're pretty smart," he has a small one-sided smile as he says this.

"My father tears my work whenever he sees it. I once wrote a sixty paged book and he sighted it and told me it was a waste of time and ripped it all up. That book took me months to write," You say slowly. You can tell he is a bit perplexed because his mouth hangs in a small o-shape, as though unbelieving. He recovers quickly enough though.

"Then you can write here…well, you can write anywhere but I give you the permission to keep your work here. You can always leave your work here in this room and pick it up whenever you want, okay?"

You nod and think of all the books you shall write.

"Let's play the piano, shall we?" he asks.

You smile. You feel like there are butterflies of happiness flying in the room – today feels heavenly. Just before school ends, Mr. Raymond slips a piece of paper into your hands. When you get home, you write in your diary:

I feel a lot better than I did yesterday night, after my parents fought.

Mr. Raymond says I would make a good writer and if he says it, then I believe it.

I'm going to start writing a new story.

I'm not sure what I'm going to write about, but I believe when I begin to write, inspiration will suddenly come.

I think I know what I want to be already: I want to be a pianist (because the happiness I feel when playing the piano is just surreal) and I'm not sure yet, but I think I'd also like to be a writer.

I'm going to write all sorts of things, starting from poems to articles to novels to award-winning plays.

I'm a dreamer – I can spend hours imagining what will never be…but it's a good thing, because, in those fleeting moments of imagining the impossible, hope overwhelms me.

I'd rather prefer to stay there, in those dreams, than to come to reality sometimes.

Today, Mr. Raymond slipped a note into my hand, and it read:

'You said to love is to suffer. I respectfully disagree. I once read a Bible passage on love - it should be 1 Corinthians 13:4-7(New International Version) – and it said:

- *Love is patient*
- *Love is kind.*
- *It does not envy.*
- *It does not boast.*
- *It is not proud.*
- *It does not dishonour others.*
- *It is not self-seeking.*
- *It is not easily angered.*
- *It keeps no record of wrongs.*
- *Love does not delight in evil but rejoices with the truth.*
- *It always protects.*
- *Always trusts.*
- *Always hopes.*
- *Always perseveres.*
- *I want you to think about it, to dwell on these words because that is what love truly should be.'*

So, Dear Diary, this is what I will think about this night before I sleep and every other night as well.

I will think of all the things love should be.

And perhaps, I will write it on a big piece of paper and paste it on the wall in the sitting room so my parents can catch a glimpse of it.

I will try also to love, to love the way it says in Mr. Raymond's note, as I should.

Testimony Odey is a Nigerian teen writer, poet, and artist. When she is not reading or writing, you can find her watching Nollywood movies or scrolling through social media, where she encourages fellow Christians and makes new friends. Her first book, Uloma, won 2nd place in the Nigeria Prize for Teen Authors 2021 (Prose Category) and is currently being published. She also participated in the maiden edition of the KepressNG Anthology Prize and won.

SISTER

Erhu Kome

Your sister is the most amazing girl in the world. No one can tell you otherwise. Her smile is bigger and brighter than anyone's, and she rarely frowns. She cooks porridge in a way that brings neighbours to your house, and she hand sews her clothes.

She reads textbooks and novels she borrows from the local library late into the night and even though you complain about the fumes of the kerosene lamp, you like to watch her read. Sometimes she cries on one page and then burst out laughing when she turns to the very next page. She says she sees the world in the books she reads. Someday she would go out to see it in person.

She is the smartest person you know. You used to think it was your father, but he did not know where Indonesia was on the map when you asked him.

Your sister knows where Indonesia is and knows the capital of every country in Asia.

The school's headmaster praises her whenever he sees your parents at church.

"Your daughter will go very far," he usually says and tilts his big round hairless head toward your sister.

Your mother and father's response never changes: "We thank God."

They come to take your sister on a rainy night. It is two hours after dinner, and she usually likes to read when it rains. Three women come into the room and your sister immediately starts to shout.

The women are people you know around the neighbourhood. They are big strong women with thick arms that jiggle around when they walk.

They grab your sister, and you join her to try to fight them. Why would they not leave her alone? Do they not see that she does not want to go with them?

But you are no match for them. And neither is she. Your sister continues to shout and call for your mother, but your mother does not come and they drag your sister away into the rainy night.

When you try to run after them, your mother finally comes to hold you back from following "Where are they taking her?" you ask them.

"She's going to get the cut. Don't worry it's not too bad. It will make her a woman. Once you are fourteen, you will get your cut too. Your girl children will too when they come of age."

You do not understand what she is saying but you have heard your sister talk about the cut and how she would rather die than have it.

Your mother leaves you in the care of your father and goes out into the night too.

You wish it is to bring your sister back, so she does not have to have the cut, but you doubt it.

Your sister does not return until two days after.

Her eyes are red and swollen and there is no life in them. She winces any time she takes a step and tears pool in her eyes when she sits down. You wait for her to speak to you, but she does not. She stays in the room you share and stares out the window most of the day.

When you can no longer take it, you bring her the book she was reading the day she was taken. She forces a smile that look strange to you, and she ignores the book.

Your sister develops a fever a few days after being home. She sweats, shakes, and trashes against the bed and you pray to God to make her stop. The medicine works for a while. But her fever comes back often.

You go to school, but she does not.

Your mother says she does not need to go to school.

Your sister does not smile any more, she does not read, and she does not speak much to you or anyone. She seems to always be in pain.

You hate your parents. You hate that they let this happen. They let this cut take your sister's spark away and what sleeps in the room with you is nothing but an empty shell.

You never want to reach age fourteen. You do

not want this cut.

You start to listen in on your parents' whispers. Your mother thinks if your sister gets pregnant, her bouts of illnesses would stop.

The man who comes to take your sister away is almost as old as your father. He has a small nose, a balding head and a split upper lip. He stares at your sister like she is a good pot of soup. Your father accepts the drink and money from him and his family.

You cry a lot during the ceremony and your mother uses her eyes to warn you to stop embarrassing them. You leave the parlour where the wedding is taking place and hide in the backyard until it is over.

And your sister is gone.

You know where your sister now lives with her husband, but you cannot bring yourself to visit. She is the third wife and is always with one of the other wives.

You spy on her on your way back from school. She looks smaller than you remember, emaciated and with no joy on her face.

Your mother talks about her a lot. She talks about how her husband regularly sends money to your father and how grateful she is. She talks about the miscarriages your sister had and weeps in a corner, so your father does not hear.

Before your fourteenth birthday, your mother comes back home from the market overjoyed. She has seen your sister's belly. This one is going to stay. Her grandchild is on the way.

You run out of the house to go see her. It is just as your mother says. Her bony body makes the belly obvious. You wonder if she is eating well. Tears run down your face and your hands quake.

You quickly wipe the tears off and run away when someone approaches.

You keep a close ear to your parents' talks. You want to be prepared for when the women come for you. You keep a knife under your pillow, and you believe you are ready to use it.

But you do not get to use it.

Your sister comes to pick you up from school one day. In her hand is a small bag.

She smiles when she sees you. The smile you had always known to be hers.

You run to hug her and feel the movement in her belly and you pray it is a boy not a girl. Your sister cries and you cry along with her.

She hastily hands you the bag and some money.

She had overheard the women were coming that night for the cutting ceremony. She says you can run away. She has prepared for you to be taken in by a nun in a town far from your village.

'They will not do to you what they did to me,' she says and despite her weary look, you see a fleck of your sister's spark again.

Erhu Kome comes from the Urhobo tribe and grew up in Benin city, so you could say she has eaten the most delicious foods in the world. She writes speculative fiction, weird stories and sometimes normal stories. She has also written shorter works that have gone on to be widely published and shortlisted for prizes. She loves anime, Bob's Burgers, and shows that have Eric Kripke involved in the making.

LOVE AT NO SIGHT

♥

Oluwatoyin M.

Ajike sits comfortably on her bed as she reminisces about her past relationship. It had been months since she had spoken to 'Mr J', her alleged boyfriend whom she met on a dating website a year ago. *Tinder* has been the solution to connecting people worldwide, and the app has produced many couples. The outbreak of the Corona Virus has brought the world to a halt, and thus, it is now difficult for people to interact physically; this has made many singles turn to the app in the hope of connecting with their soul mate, or maybe just a one-night stand.

All these sound like excuses to Kemisola, Ajike's roommate. She believes Ajike is just too shy to meet boys, so thus turns to the app to seek love without being seen. None of these are lies. In fact, Ajike has never been in a relationship; she has not had her first kiss yet.

Unlike Ajike, Kemisola is known to be a beautiful, sensual, intelligent, top-notch bachelorette at their university. However, her beauty is seen through her makeup. If she and Ajike were to compete in a beauty pageant without wearing makeup, Ajike would win. Ajike is that one simple girl who stands out with or without makeup. She wishes for a percent of Kemisola's confidence.

Kemisola could woo men to her without a word. Her whole appearance says, 'I'm the one.' Although she has no knowledge of fashion or a background in styling, Instagram has been a friend of hers for a long time; she would look up styles and trends online and, in return, copy them. She is known to be a trendsetter, and most campus girls choose her as their style icon.

Even with her popularity, Kemisola still chooses to be friends with Ajike. She feels safe with Ajike, unlike any girl on campus, and they would do anything to protect each other. They never break each other's girl code, such as talking bad behind each other, or snatching each other's boyfriend. Or maybe Kemisola knows Ajike couldn't talk to boys, or Ajike is too loyal to try.

"Are you still brooding over this matter?" Kemisola asked when she saw Ajike lost in thought. She has tried multiple times to console her best friend over the matter. She had even given a warning not to fall in love with strangers on the internet.

"Most boys you see online have one hidden girlfriend or two, they just wanted to meet new girls with the purpose of a one-night stand."

"But he should at least tell me the reason why he is not responding to my texts anymore?" Ajike cried *while resting her head on Kemisola's shoulder.*

'Mr J' to Ajike has been a comforter, although they've never met, they chatted and exchanged pictures online. Looking through their texts, one could sense love and affection, he was a charmer, a sweetheart, one that melted the heart of Ajike. His profile pictures predict him to be a normal-looking guy, not handsome, still not ugly. But he is generally a sweetheart throughout the conversation he exchanged with Ajike.

"But you too should have known him to be trouble the moment he refused to let you video call him. What kind of man won't allow video calls?" Kemisola was worried that her best friend had fallen for a catfisher. She had watched numerous shows on television about it.

"Do you think he is back in Nigeria? Last time we communicated, he told me he was in Russia. Maybe that's why he is not responding to my texts…" Ajike said, trying to make excuses for her online boyfriend. When you're in love, you just make things up in your head even though you may sound stupid.

"Russia kor? North Korea ni? Abeg, stop trying to cover up for him. You should have known from the start that he is 4.1.9. He even made up lies about being in Russia? Wonders shall never end nowadays!" Kemisola blurted out in annoyance, already fed up with the stories and lies. She just wished her friend would stop being a child and

move on. But still, she understands that this is Ajike's first time experiencing heartbreak. So, she decided to wait up on her and help her as friends do.

"We were supposed to meet a year from now. He promised to take our relationship to the next level and promised to take me home." Ajike griped. "He told me he loves me, that I'm different from other girls. He told me I'm beautiful and unique, so why is he not responding to my text messages?" Ajike inquired, and Kemisola listened like a mother consoling her child.

'And he said all these over a text, yet he broke up with you?' Kemisola mocked silently. She wanted to share some good news with Ajike, but she couldn't, not when her friend still mourned.

⁂

After a week of constant resentment and heartbreak, Ajike pulls herself together and decides to wait. She still believes that one day she'll meet 'Mr J', and both will fall in love. She attended lectures with a happy mind and won't get distracted by the constant stares the boys in her department gave her. Although she is beautiful and lacks confidence, she believes Kemisola is more beautiful and is not ready to share the spotlight with her, nor is she ready to date boys casually as Kemisola does. She believes in true love and soul mates. She doesn't see a reason in casual dating if there is no love behind it, coming from someone who has fallen in love at no sight.

"I've got a surprise for you!" Kemisola screamed; she had been meaning to tell Ajike for a while and now's the right time.

"What is it again? New boyfriend?" Ajike mocked. Kemisola a.k.a. was a fisher of men; she changed boyfriend like she changed clothes. Every rich and handsome guy on campus would have gone out with her if care was not taken. She couldn't even recount the numbers of girls on campus who had come knocking and demanding the release of their boyfriends.

"You've guessed right, but even better. I met a guy three weeks ago."

"And?" Ajike quizzed with high hope. She believed her friend had caught a big fish this time.

"He is charming, good-looking, rich, and most importantly he is far better than those chicken-change boys on campus. He is five years older than us which makes him sexier," Kemisola replied coyly.

"So, he is twenty-seven years old? And are you sure he is not a fraudster?"

Kemisola giggled. "Not everyone that is older is a fraud. Plus, we've met physically, and he is the kind of guy every lady dreams of. I can't believe he asked me out. It was as if we knew each other or had met before. I'm starting to believe in true love like you." All the boys she had dated on campus are mostly good-looking but generally not well *blessed.* To finally find a guy wealthy enough to care for her needs and desires was truly worth celebrating.

"Hallelujah! Finally!! Congratulations!!"

Ajike had her own worries, but her friend had found love. Although it made her more vulnerable, she must be happy for Kemisola.

"I want you to meet him this weekend. He is holding a house party here in Lekki. And I want you to come with me, maybe you can find yourself a new man that can replace your heartbreak," Kemisola replied. She wanted to take Ajike along so as to brag about her man, and also be able to find Ajike a new guy - like killing two birds with one stone.

"Are you sure it's okay for me to tag along? I would rather prefer to stay at home."

"So, you can numb your pain? Abeg, you have no choice but to follow me. You want me to go all the way to Lekki all alone? And you call yourself my best friend?" Kemisola complained.

Now, Ajike has no choice but to follow her and become a third wheel for the day. Although she has no desire to meet a new guy yet, or maybe not physically, she is certain that 'Mr J' is real, and when she finds him, she will be ready to do everything to make him hers. She wouldn't mind asking him out if only he would respond to her messages.

"Or maybe something happened to him? What if he had lost his phone? Or is he sick? Or maybe dead?" Ajike pondered.

Saturday arrived as quickly as expected. The girls have already planned for the weekend, their outfits and shoes. Kemisola wants to be the jewel of the party, and also be able to turn heads. She may be young, but she believes in her youthful look to *slay* in the party.

On the other hand, Ajike prefers to be comfortable in her own skin. She couldn't care less about wearing makeup or choosing the best outfit since her intention was not to party or make friends; she was a tag-along anyway.

As planned, the Uber arrives, taking the girls to a gigantic mansion in Lekki. Lekki is one of the areas in Lagos, Nigeria, that has housed millionaires and billionaires; the movers and shakers of Lagos have made Lekki their home. The beautiful scenery and exquisite real estate in the area attract people from around the continent and make them settle down. Guys like Kemisola's new boyfriend are wealth personified.

The girls appear taken aback when they first enter the mansion. The interior screams wealth and power, and without being fully aware, they start feeling small in the presence of everyone around them. Full of overflowing confidence, Kemisola mingles with the children of important personalities and a high network, but Ajike doesn't dare say a word to those people.

The man of the moment arrives wearing a

Versace overall. He is just as Kemisola had portrayed. He is even far better looking than the picture Kemisola had painted for Ajike. His gentle smile melts the hearts of everyone. From a distance, Ajike admires him like she has met him before but cannot remember how or when. When he comes closer to her, she feels some sort of familiarity and deep connection, but she is able to control herself and not mess things up for her friend.

"Hi! You must be Ajike, Kemisola's roommate and best friend. Nice meeting you! I'm Jamal." He stretches out his long arm for a handshake.

"Nice meeting me, I mean nice meeting you!" Ajike stutters, unable to control herself around him. She can't sense why, but since the guy in front of her belongs to Kemisola, she wouldn't dare to dream of having him, but she could enjoy the moment of conversation between them.

"I hope you girls are enjoying yourself, my house is your house," he says comfortably.

"Is this your house?" Kemisola questions while staying close to him as if marking her man to keep others away from him.

"Actually, my parents' house. Or should I say our parents' house. My brother and I live in this house, but our parents chose to stay at Banana Island, because it's more secure and safe."

"You have a brother?"

"I do, you will meet him very soon. Oh! Here he comes."

A gentleman walks awkwardly towards them. His appearance has a great effect on Ajike, especially as she realizes that the man walking towards them looks exactly like the man she had been waiting for all along. Could he be 'Mr J'? She thinks to herself. But as he walks up close enough to her, she now certainly believes that he is truly Mr J.

"Mr J?"

Both men are taken aback on hearing the name as if they were aware of who 'Mr J' might be.

"Do you know him?"

Jamal questions enthusiastically.

"Not really, he looks like someone I know. I'm sorry, will you please excuse me?" Ajike stomps out at full speed.

Kemisola wonders what could have gone wrong, so she followed her. It is strange enough that Ajike calls out 'Mr J', but why would she run out?

"What is wrong with you? Why do you have to leave like that?" Kemisola asks, looking concerned.

"That's 'Mr J' in there. The guy I told you about, the one that broke my heart. He is your boyfriend's brother."

"You don't mean it? So why are you not saying anything? You could have taken the chance to get to know him? This is a big opportunity for you."

"I can't!"

"Why can't you?"

It turns out Ajike used Kemisola's pictures for her

dating profile, and the man inside would think Kemisola was the girl he has fallen for. Now everything is going awry more than she had expected. She confesses.

"Are you insane? You used my pictures to communicate with a guy? Have you gone mad, Ajike? Why would you do such a thing? You know I'm dating his brother, how on earth am I supposed to face two brothers now?" Kemisola snapps. She knows how shy Ajike is, but not up to the level of impersonating her to chat with boys.

"I just thought if he saw your pictures, he would like you better than I do. And it worked, he fell for me… for you."

"What am I supposed to do now? You better pray he doesn't remember my face, if not I will sue you. But why would you do such a thing, Ajike?"

"I hope so too. What should I do now?"

Kemisola couldn't think of anything. All she wants is to be with a new boyfriend, not his regular-looking brother.

"Let's go in first. I'm sure we can go with the flow," she reassures her, and both went back in. Throughout the day, 'Mr J' never takes a glance at Kemisola, but he seemed to have his attention on Ajike. He would walk up to her to offer her a drink and use the opportunity to have a conversation with her. He introduces himself as James, the introverted brother

Although their conversations throughout the day

were unlike the ones they chatted through texts, Ajike appeared a little open to him. She felt safe in his presence; he was like a brother figure to her—not what she expected, but cool. She was bothered by the fact that he didn't recognize Kemisola and why he chose her instead.

"Your friend knows my brother?" Jamal asks after witnessing the closeness between James and Ajike. He felt a little bothered but couldn't figure out why.

"It's a long story," Kemisola commented.

***

Through the night, Jamal tosses around in bed. He feels uneasy, like someone who had been caught cheating. A year ago, he was lonely after breaking up with his then-girlfriend who had cheated on him with his best friend, he went online using his brother's dating account to meet girls to numb his pain. He wants a girl who fell for his sincerity, not someone after his money or handsome-looking face. By using his brother's profiles, he was able to meet Kemisola, she turned the world around for him. He fell deeply in love with her, she was different and special.

From their chats, she is humble and kind, but meeting her physically he could sense something was wrong. He feels more attracted to Ajike, but he can't figure out why. Seeing his brother closer to Ajike during the party angered him, he was jealous of them without knowing why. He gets out of his bed, pacing, remembering her face like a portrait in his head, even though he had forgotten how Kemisola looked, but Ajike's face is what keeps popping in his head.

"She has a gorgeous smile by the way," he says out loud, without thinking.

"Who has a gorgeous smile?" James asks, noticing his brother's unease when he enters his room.

"Can't you knock? You scared me!"

"I did, but you were so lost in thought, you couldn't hear me! What is making you so jumpy? Is it the girl you brought to the party? She is beautiful, I know she is your type, but I like her friend much better. She was charming and she is even beautiful compared to your girlfriend."

Jamal becomes more tense when he hears James's interest in Ajike, the thought of them being together doesn't sit well with him. He feels like kidnapping her and taking her far away from everyone. He believes Ajike belongs to him, but how?

"But something is strange. She called me, 'Mr J' earlier. Have we met before? It's not like we did, but how could she know I'm called, 'Mr J'? Maybe it's destiny," James assures himself.

"Destiny my foot. Do you believe in destiny?" Jamal replies in annoyance. It was clear that Kemisola knew 'Mr J', Ajike's alleged online boyfriend. But when he met with Kemisola, she was oblivious of him or maybe it appeared so.

On the other hand, Kemisola still questioned Ajike on what the two talked about.

"So, did he say he recognized me?"

"Not really, but he never even mentioned your name. This is still new to me, so all this while he was not paying attention to me... to you," Ajike complained.

"When I'm telling you men are scums, you won't believe me. Imagine how he denied ever seeing you or should I say me? I know for sure my Jamal is not like that. He is so charming and too handsome for that."

She daydreams about him before realizing he hasn't called her yet. She contemplates calling him first, but she never dares to so as not to be seen as desperate.

'Men love women who are not clingy' - this is the rule she had set for herself when dating.

"How about I ask Jamal if we could go on a double date, maybe you and James can get closer? What do you think?"

Kemisola is over the moon in a new relationship. It may be unknown to her, but she has fallen for Jamal. He is everything she has imagined.

"I don't think I'm ready for dating yet, you and Jamal can go on your date. I'm fine!" Ajike replies, concealing the fact that she has taken a liking to Jamal; if Kemisola finds out, she might be in real trouble, so she keeps things to herself.

"Look at you, why don't you take the chance of getting closer to your dream man? Or are you not the same person dying here some days back? Don't you want to know why he stopped talking to you?" Kemisola queries.

What's on Ajike's mind is far from the flings she has with James via chatting. She could sense a connection between her and Jamal more than with James. It would be better if she never stays close to Jamal, or her heart would pound like a beating drum again.

"Okay, if you insist, I will join you guys." Ajike silently hopes to see Jamal again, so she will take the chance of seeing him again.

"That's better!"

***

"You are looking suspicious!" Kemisola teases Ajike after seeing her face made up.

Ajike has taken full consideration into her outfits. She appears more beautiful than Kemisola, one would think it was her birthday. For the first time, she wears a short dress, with little cleavage exposed, showing off her legs. One who hasn't met her before or is not close to her would think she is a totally different person. Her whole appearance screamed: confident. And for the first time, Kemisola feels overshadowed. Although she wouldn't dare tell Ajike to appear less beautiful so as not to step on her ego she lets it go, but she would also appear as good as her friend.

"Are you sure I'm not doing too much?" Ajike asks, feeling a little overwhelmed by her own appearance.

"You look good, Friend. I'm sure if James sees what he has been missing all along, he will fall without tripping!" Kemisola assures Ajike.

James? Ajike didn't dress up to look good for James, she dressed up to get Jamal's attention. She wouldn't mind meeting him alone, but she still wants him to think of her as being beautiful.

What happened to the good girl Ajike? It is like Jamal is turning her into a bad girl. It is not a bad thing, but it would be disaster if Kemisola finds out that she has a crush on her man.

"Let's go, before we keep the guys waiting for too long!"

The girls hurriedly leave the hostel to catch an Uber. Their date is in a reserved park. They planned to walk hand in hand and admire wild animals and the amazing natural environment.

Upon seeing the new Ajike, both boys' hearts dropped like they were starstruck; it's as if they'd seen an angel in human form. Kemisola doesn't get the huge compliment which makes her jealous. She gets mad at her boyfriend for eyeing Ajike as she is supposed to be his date, but Jamal is acting as if he wishes Ajike is his date. Kemisola knew something was wrong with Jamal from the party. It was as if Ajike and Jamal already knew each other. Maybe they were pretending not to know each other.

"You're so beautiful, do you know that?" James says out loud in the presence of the three. He gives a compliment without being shy for the first time. He even hands a rose to Ajike, which Jamal couldn't think of getting for Kemisola.

Jamal is more curious about Ajike than Kemisola. He wants to spend time alone with her without any distraction or tag-along. He wants to ask her what her favourite food is, what she likes to do when she is free, and what kind of songs she listens to.

"How about we see the lion first?" Kemisola suggests to break the awkwardness between them, but she is ignored as Jamal walks to Ajike and asks if she wants to see the alligators with him.

"I don't think it's well-mannered for you to be asking my date out?" James snaps.

Feeling a little intimidated by the situation and not wanting to cause a ruckus between the two brothers or break her friendship code, Ajike requests, "How about we all just go see the alligators together?"

"Let's do that, Ajike," Kemisola says to save the day. Jamal had been acting funny to her, so she would do what Jamal wants to stay on his good terms.

Finally, they all agree to see the alligators. As everyone watches the alligators, Jamal has his eyes on Ajike the whole time. When their eyes meet, Ajike feels a rush of adrenaline. She can only bite her lips to control herself, even as she imagines them kissing, which makes the thought stronger and harder to resist, so she has no choice but to run from his presence.

"Why are you avoiding me?" Jamal asks when they are alone again - their dates has gone to buy some refreshments.

"No. I'm not! Why do you think so?" Ajike stutters, keeping away from him.

"Do I do something wrong? You are acting indifferent to me suddenly!"

"No, you don't. It's because you're too handsome!" Ajike mumbles without thinking. *What the hell?* 'Too handsome'. *What will he think of me?*

Jamal smiles brightly as he realizes that Ajike also finds him attractive. He had dressed up to get recognition from her.

"You're too beautiful for me to handle likewise!" Jamal replies, feeling good.

He felt a rush down his spine suddenly, his mind telling him to stop but his whole body encouraging him; he gets close to her and in no time kisses her.

It is a magical moment for Ajike; it is her first kiss ever, and she is doing it with someone she loves.

Unknown to them, James and Kemisola have witnessed the whole thing.

Oluwatoyin Magbagbeola is a twenty-three-year-old Nigerian who's very passionate about storytelling. She's driven and motivated by African literature and poetry, and most importantly, loves the element and art of her culture. Being an African is my identity, and I'm super proud to be a Nigerian. She hopes to inspire others to read and explore my imaginative mind. She writes about African history, food, lifestyle, and culture for the Afrovibe magazine.

MOTHER'ED MY GIRLS

Chibuike Agbalokwu

The night was silenced by the immense darkness; the moon had found its way to its lover's bed, leaving the night in the hand of nothing, not even the wind. I wasn't sure what woke me up – my dream or the hot night. I was sweating terribly.

I used my wrapper, which was loosely held to my body, to wipe my forehead. I contemplated throwing the wrapper away, but my last child will always remind me of her presence in the room. She would turn and sleep-talk, beckoning her sleep friends. Most of what she says eludes me. Not only that, but I would also be a feast to the whining mosquitoes. Else, I would have thrown away the mosquito net too. The nets felt like fiery confinement inside my already small apartment.

A dog barked from a distance continuously. The bark heralded the loud screech coming from a machete being scratched against a hard surface. It came suddenly, and it startled me. I knew it was the local vigilante guarding the street, but I never got used to their noise. Even though they had been around for years and had continuously disturbed our night with either the machete, the whistle, or their chants. We pay through our nose for us to sleep peacefully, but we have only gotten nuisance. The noise was an assurance to other residents but never to me.

"What is it?" my husband asked in a calm, throaty voice. I jumped. I didn't know he was awake.

"Chi'm," I exclaimed. I had to hold my chest with my hand to steady my heart which was racing. I had sat up on the bed. "I wake you? Sorry."

"I don wake for the past thirty minutes. You are turning again in bed, pushing and kicking like sey you get bad dream."

His voice was lovely and calm. I couldn't trace any sign of anger, and it was greatly fulfilling. It was an assurance that he still loved me. I wiped my face again with my wrapper, thinking of what to say.

"You were calling Chioma again and again," he said.

My response was a series of stuttered incoherent words, but I made sure to let him know it was not a dream but rather, the heat. He didn't respond to my gibberish but rather dragged me gently to lie down. He had heard that response a thousand and one times. He untied my wrapper and pulled it down to my waist.

I protested in my heart; our children might wake up anytime. He cladded me with his body. The worst thing that could happen this night was sex. I hadn't made up my mind to refuse yet, but he produced a hand fan and started fanning me. I gave a silent thanksgiving prayer. I couldn't believe I let him know the name of my last child. My last dead baby.

Chioma will always come to me in my dreams. One time, she would want to suckle at my breast, another time she would want me to cuddle her to sleep, other times she would just want to be around me. But she always comes crying and wouldn't stop until I gave in to her yearnings.

There were days, if not most of the days, I wouldn't want anything to do with her, but she would not go away. I might beat her or kick her, my poor little baby, but she would keep on coming back. Her scream drives me crazy. I rarely slept well. What kind of a baby would not let her mother know any rest? Sometimes, I wonder how it would have been had she lived.

The morning came with its refreshing air. The very few minutes after waking up that reminds one of sweet nature. Chills of heavenly dew and breath of eternal bliss just before reality sets in. I call it dawn of reality and mine creeps in the way dirty water tints a clear one upon mixture. The usual frown beguiled my face. The type that always got Obinna to laugh.

My sweet husband. My love for him never diminished despite what he made me go through. In our early years, he would be there to kiss away my anguish. He will then make sweet promises to me about how our life will get better someday. How our girls will marry rich husbands and our boys will have enough to inherit. In his breath of roses and promises, I would draw strength and joy to face yet another day.

Today, he was not there despite my drowning sorrow.

The dawn of reality came with a sudden nausea. Who does not have the horror of vomit? My stomach churned terribly. I ran out to the gutter outside and vomited. I hadn't eaten much last night and had little to throw up. It was mid-morning; therefore, most of our neighbours have gone out. I touched my neck to discover I was running a temperature. I swallowed hard. My heart raced. The feeling was nostalgic, and I dreaded it. I never forgot any single day, nor did I forget all the atrocities I did to Chioma. I felt myself falling.

E gburu m Chioma oo! I killed Chioma! I killed my baby!

Strong arms grabbed me by the elbow. I had gone swindling, almost falling into the big dirty gutter where all the dirty water from the bathrooms and kitchens in the compound pass through. It must have been Iya Ibeji. I couldn't care less but trusted the arm to lead me to safety. My landing was soft, and I guessed I was eased onto my bed. I fell asleep. Later on, I noticed my body had been wiped with a wet warm towel. I slept off again.

★★★

Chioma placed her head on my stomach. She was smiling. I touched her hair; she's already a year old, and her entangled and unkempt hair should be shaved off. She kept on smiling. She placed her hands over her mouth to hush me. She was peaceful, unlike what she had always been. It was like she was listening to my stomach. Suddenly, she started screaming and hitting me. She dug her nails into my skin and scratched. The pain was splintering. For the first time, I hit her. The blow was so hard that she fell off. I feared I had hurt her, but it didn't deter her. She came running back to me. I was screaming as I was trying to push her off.

Iya Ibeji tried to hold me down as I fought her. It was mortifying when I discovered she was at the receiving end of my tantrums. Filled with shame, I started sobbing. She consoled me. I know she was sure I took in again, and her pity must have been from the fact that my last baby was stillborn. Nobody sympathised with a baby killer. She didn't know I killed my baby. The food she bought from my favourite joint was not able to go down my throat. I slept off again.

I woke up to the ululating children as they made their way into the house. I jumped to my feet. It felt like I had forgotten to breathe. I felt like a stranger in my own world. I hadn't done anything that day, and the children would be hungry. Their father gives them money to sort themselves out in the morning. It's almost dark, and I have no plans for dinner. My body felt terribly weak, but that wouldn't count for anything. My family must be served. I pushed our cranky door aside to head for the kitchen which was situated outside the building.

To my surprise, I saw my husband having a hushed conversation with Iya Ibeji. Looks like that type of conversation a son has with the mother-in-law that results in him divorcing his wife. Many questions crossed my mind. Iya Beji is not my mother-in-law, but she might as well be putting in words for her. Here, no one minds their business. Then again, had she faced her business, I might still be lying in my own vomit outside.

Obinna looked at me and smiled. They concluded the conversation and he approached me. Iya beji called out to me before heading to her room. Obinna placed his strong arms around me. I felt his warm strong arms. I perceived his perfume which was mixed with sweat. Just the right dose that drives me crazy. I fell into his arms. His love mattered to me.

"You shouldn't disturb yourself. We will buy mama-put for the night," he said.

"Excuse me," said Iyene, one of our neighbours. Obviously, we were blocking her path to the kitchen. I felt bad for displaying such affection where she can see us. It felt almost like a spite because she was yet to be married and she was well beyond the proper age. The thought amused me, for even though I felt bad for her, I might still bring it up next time we start quarrelling on who messed up the shared toilet.

We continued on our way back to our room, holding hands. I am pregnant, and it scared me. I guess that was the reason Chioma fought me after some moment of peace. I would still want my days of peace. I don't want the anxiety of not knowing if the baby would be a boy or a girl. The thought of what I might pass through made me want to convulse. I tried to keep it off my heart till I would have to go to the hospital.

With his hands gently patting my back and the sweetest of voices, he said, "It will surely be a boy."

My heart melted, and I could taste my bile in my mouth. The horror he made me go through was because he couldn't have a girl for his fifth child. Even the takeout food he bought from a fast-food joint did little to cheer me up. I felt downtrodden.

★★★

It started out as an argument. I was afraid he will ask me to leave his house after the hospital told me I will give birth to a girl. My mind would run into a frenzy anytime his mother called him. I lived in fear. He was the only son of his parents, and it was only customary he continued his lineage by giving birth to a son. I waited for him to drop the bombshell, but he never did.

That cold night, he whispered to my ears how he would want me to give him a son. He loved me terribly and would not let me go despite the advice from his mother and friends. He promised he would not humiliate me by going outside to another lady. I felt his love that night and we cried together.

However, he told me he cannot bear any more expensse for a girl. We were feeding from hand to mouth already. He told me to do everything I can to get rid of the baby, or better still, kill her in my stomach. The Ogbuefi Foundation will see to my operation. They would not give in to abortion because it is illegal, and even if they did, he won't have them risk spoiling my womb because I will still bear him a son.

I agreed to all he said because he iterated the fact that he still loved me. I had to do what I had to do to get rid of the baby. Hence, my horror began.

Early morning, I would line up with the agberos, hoodlums, in my street to take agbo, herbal medicine, mixed with gin. I would take more of it to the extent of intoxication. When the vendor raised her concern, I would lie and brag that I took it when I was pregnant with my four daughters, and they came out fine. My baby would shift uncomfortably but my heart was set on stone.

Was it my love for Obinna? Or the fact that I want to remain married? Or pure naivete? I cannot tell, but I cannot imagine a life without Obinna and a family. What will people say?

Intentionally, I would jump the stairs in front of our building. I did this when no one was looking. Being of great height, I always land with my hands to the ground. I would bear the terrible pain that would jolt to my waist. If I felt like this, I wondered how my baby had felt. I wept every night.

The grief wouldn't stop me from sleeping without a mosquito net. I had malaria drugs more than four times before I was due. The sickness made me so gloomy and pale. People will ask me the reason why I haven't been to the hospital, and I will lie that it had always been like this whenever I am pregnant.

Later on, my husband will bring back some concoction. He said that it will make sure all my efforts were not in vain. He assured me that this is the only way we both get what we want. He wouldn't want any quack doctor to spoil my womb in the name of abortion.

Obinna would kiss me on my neck before reminding me that I am the only one he wanted to bear his children. His love for me knew no bounds. He knew how to hypnotise me. I would hold him so tightly amidst pain and passion.

Even though the concoction might be causing an unknown amount of pain in my stomach, I had comfort. Most night, with my consent, he would slip inside me. To be truthful, nothing could ease my pain, both his presence made me believe I am suffering for a cause and that we are in it together.

The labour came in earlier than I expected. The pain was excruciating. I wept bitterly when I noticed because I was sure my baby was dead. At that point, I realized what I had done. I drowned myself in the pain as a sort of mortification, but nothing could make up for what I did to her. I wanted to name her Chioma. I don't know when I did, but that was what I called her. The doctor was so furious. He was right when he said I killed my child, but it wasn't carelessness; it was intentional.

I had been moody and angry ever since that day. I fought everybody that crossed me. The nights weren't any easier. Initially, it was all bliss with Chioma. She suckled my breast; I would wake up with a soaked cloth. It all went bad when I started to resent her. She would cry all through the night. Although I slept, I had no rest. It became worse now that I am pregnant.

★★★

A passer-by smiled at me as I sat alone on the long bench of the hospital. The maternity ward was the only part of a hospital where you get to experience joy. Nobody is dying, just humans happy to bring another angel into the world. Women with protruding stomachs and men with food flasks, flowers, and love. There I was, amidst so much happiness, but sad. No one knew I came to the hospital. No one needed to know that I have inquired about the sex of my baby. The nurse had smiled when she said it was a girl. Little did she know she was breaking bad news to me. My husband had been all love and affection, but this was the kind of news that could turn him into a monster. A sweet monster, nonetheless. I sobbed. The thought of murdering my baby again made me nauseous. I ran outside to the gutter and vomited.

That night, I cried all through. Obinna still made love to me when the kids slept off. He fell asleep immediately after he released. I slept too.

★★★

Chioma had a mean face. I pushed her away immediately I saw her. She struggled to reach me, scratching and screaming. My slippers came handy. The beatings did not stop her from attacking me though. At some point, I was trying to prevent her from killing my baby. She was just a year old, when I flung her, she flew a great distance before hitting her head on the concrete floor. My heart sank to my stomach. The floor was soon dripping in her blood. I screamed to my wake.

No one woke up, or they were used to my commotion and wouldn't lose a night's sleep. The dream was gory, and the headache that visited me was splintering. I held my head and with a hushed, scared voice I iterated, "Chi m oo". I don't know if Chioma will cease to visit me now that I have murdered her the second time, but at that moment, I decided that I will not kill my children again. Come what may. I laid down again, but sleep didn't come. I remembered I am yet to eat. There was a plate of rice by my bed. I had hoped to eat it at midnight since I had no appetite that evening. I scooped a spoon, but it did not go down my throat. I am running away with my baby girls. If my family reject me, I will find elsewhere but never in the house of a murderer.

Obinna woke me up with kisses. He fumbled my breast and brushed my hips with his. The soft words he spoke drizzled like early morning dew. I opened

120

my mouth to tell him off but instead, I said:
    "She's a girl."

LOVE LIKE BLOOMING VINE

Obianuju Jane Ebubeoha

Love, I've heard grows like a blooming vine. Slow at first it sprouts, but nurtured with patience and care, it steadily spreads its warmth like the Cypress on a powder-white trellis, adding colour and light to our lives.

It felt like a tale carved out of folklore which was made up by silly, old elderlies to preach love and patience to little, oblivious children because I know better and have learned my lesson the hard way. The reformed me was smarter and more vigilant, ready to squash any distractions with the heel of my Louboutin.

This was the resolution I made as the double doors swung open from the inside to grant me access into the visitor's area of the colourful and brightly lit, pristine office.

"Mr. Felix will be with you in a moment, Miss Anne. Please make yourself comfortable," the smiling young lady at the receptionist desk with Ella boldly scrawled on the name tag across her chest.

I nod, acknowledging her words while shoving

aside thoughts about men and the devious ways they crawl under one's skin without notice, only to rip dump you in the ditch for the smooth ride. I needed to bring my A-game to the table if I intended to scale through the final stages of this interview.

Ella ushered me inside. "You've got this girl. Just be yourself," she whispered, with a small smile before shutting the door behind me.

"Miss Anne Thompson, welcome to our first physical meeting. I must say, you're quite taller in person. Please have a seat."

I tentatively took my seat, replying, "There is no law that forbids tall girls from becoming great accountants. Not even the rookie ones."

"Great sense of humour too, Miss Anne. Good to know." Adjusting his small frame into his seat, it felt more like I was towering over Mr. Felix instead of the other way around, but before he could continue, the door to his office burst open, and in walked the seduction in a suit.

My jaws dropped wide open. Staring for a full, heart-stopping second at the candy pop that just waltzed into my life-changing meeting – discarding the silent resolution I made only minutes ago – I didn't realise Mr. Felix has said something until he flashed those pearly whites in return.

I melted away in my seat; the burning desire to reach up and fist my fingers into his coal dark hair was a temptation too strong to resist and my ticket out of here if as much as lifted a finger.

It would be the creepiest thing I have ever done. Thank goodness I was the queen of restraint or else, I would be dusting my application from the rack I just dumped it two weeks ago.

"Sorry sir, I didn't realize you were in a meeting. I'll drop this final draft of the payment slip with you, so, you can go through it later and endorse it before we push it out to the bank," seduction in a suit said – his name tag was missing – to Mr. Felix.

"Drop it on my desk, Franklin, and do well to knock next time before barging into my office; we don't want guests to think we act unprofessionally here," he said, trying hard to hide his smile, same as Franklin, who gave a curt nod and a tight-lipped reply before leaving.

I was already anticipating the thrill of working here if my guess was right, and he was also an accountant. The bitch slap I got from my inner self drew my wandering thoughts back to reality, the devastating events of the last two weeks returning with a vengeance.

My eyes stung when those buried feelings rushed up to the surface, but I managed to hide them before it ruined my day and opportunity at a fresh start. I know I vowed to keep off the male gender for a long time; hell, I'm changing jobs because of it, but I couldn't help but notice the fuzzy feeling in my stomach when Franklin walked in.

Dismissing it as just nerves, I gave my full attention to Mr. Felix who seemed oblivious to my inner turmoil and bland responses to his open-ended questions, which was fine with me, seeing as I didn't have it in me to explain why my cheery disposition minutes ago has suddenly turned sour.

"You did well Miss Anne and I'm impressed with the level of composure you've shown so far. We sometimes have to work under high pressure, and I have no reservations about your ability to deliver. Your resume, although sparse, speaks highly of your acquired knowledge in the profession, which is something I can work with, and you can nurture. How would you like to start Monday?

The wide triumphant smile that broke out after that was the kind that said, *'in your face Robert, I did it without you.'*

"Monday works just fine for me," I said, extending my hands as I stood to accept his congratulatory handshake as we stood.

He drummed his fingers on the wide desk between us – I presumed he was sceptical – staring hard at my file. My heart thumped a little, getting all superstitious about something bad happening just after one gets such good news.

Well, I have my friend Vanessa to blame for that silly thought. What could go wrong, after scaling through to the end?

Everything apparently when he asked, "why did you

leave Landley Pharmaceuticals with barely six months on the job? Seems odd to me that you resigned from such a lucrative position. Is it a story worth adding to your file or personal?"

If by 'story *worth adding to my file'* he meant typing out my experience of getting used by the person I thought meant the world to me and had my back, after which he threw me under the bus to be crushed, on a piece of paper to be scrutinized all over again, then it'd be a hard pass.

At least, I was lucky not to have that dent on my permanent record. It's a miracle I will forever be grateful for. Imagine having to explain to a million and one potential employers, that I was played for a fool because I was blindly in love and trusted wholly without upholding the ethics of my profession.

The emotional turmoil would have had me crawling into a deep, dark hole to spend the rest of my days until I withered away in misery.

Choosing to opt for the obvious option, I replied with all the confidence I could muster, "It's personal sir, nothing worthy of note. I decided to leave Landley and that decision doesn't affect the position offered to me here in any way."

"Good to know. How about I show you around the facility while we give Miss Ella a few minutes to get your starter pack ready. Everything you need to know about us is expressly stated. Make sure to read through the handbooks provided within and study every inch of the professional code of ethics. You will need to master it if you want to flourish in this company."

I nod again, mentally creating a checklist of all the important stuff he just mentioned as we made our way out of his office and stepped outside the restricted area of the facility, only meant for senior executive staff.

"Welcome to Velocity World."

★★★

The next month passed by in a rush. My work hours were lined with intense facility training during the day and in-house grooming in the evening by my colleagues, who over time have grown on me because of how seemingly easy they've made my transition, despite how demanding their daily routines are.

The good news was, it didn't take me long to get a hang of the intricate interconnectivity of the operations in Velocity while the agonizing news is, the work hours were killing me and I was burning out barely a month of the job, with little sleep to aid my plight.

I was exhausted most mornings, dragging my feet out of the bed at the crack of dawn and returning home after mama calls. A new girl in a new city with no friends or family to lean on and vent about my day made it more irritable to handle and my pristine self-restraint was beginning to wane as days counted into months.

"Here, have this. You look exhausted," the light

baritone of the only male occupant in the room with me said, handing over a brown paper-covered package.

I'll be damned. He speaks. Halleluiah.

The temptation was too high not to notice. Accepting the package, with a raised brow and quirked lips for effect, I said, "I thought I was invincible. Thankfully, now I know I wasn't Sue Storm, walking around with magical powers I didn't know I had."

His knitted brows had me smiling at his confusion. "You also proved you're not a die-hard Marvel fan."

"Forgive me but you'll have to be more expressive," he said, turning to face me.

"Never mind," I said, unboxing the item inside and giggled out loud. "Am I looking that desperate in need of help?"

He shrugged, still staring hard at me, "I do know how I felt when I started here a few years back and believe you must feel the same way too. It's an energy drink but it's wrapped because we aren't supposed to drink on the job, but you need it to stop yawning every five minutes. It grows louder by the second."

My curled fist punched him in the shoulders before I could stop myself, laughing at his pitiful attempt to joke with my alarming situation. He was right though. I needed all the pro tips I could get –

even if I had to break a few rules first.

"You know we are being watched right? I mean the control room is right opposite this door and they can burst in any moment," I said, chiding him.

"Yeah, I know. Trust me, Anne, no one is bursting in to lay claims on a rule violation. We know how hard it can get, so, we get a few free passes once in a while. House rules."

Oh. What exactly have I been missing?

Popping the cover of the predator energy drink, I gulped down half the content in one swift swig and wiped my lips, bringing my gaze to meet his amused once.

"What?

"Just thinking, I should have gotten two from the mart."

"Don't be ridiculous and thank you for getting me this in the first place. My feet and back are killing me. In my last place of work, I did shifts with another accountant and still complained about the work hours. This, however, makes me want to ask for forgiveness for running my mouth carelessly. That was a heavenly bliss compared to this."

He stood, running a hand through his hair like he wanted to say something but at the same time didn't want to say it. So, I urged him on. It was the first time we were having a conversation that didn't end with mono-syllabic replies and curt nods, I wasn't about to let it get awkward.

I may be sworn off men, but a good conversation, I'd kill for any day.

"Anne, I don't mean to be forward, but if you want to know how to lay off on the stress a little bit, you need to start making a few adjustments. The girls may not tell you, to avoid overstepping their boundaries, but you do need help to wage this war properly and win."

"Oh! I didn't know I signed up for a battle. Don't see any swords and spears lying around, do you?" I asked with a tight face devoid of emotions and burst out laughing when he gaped at me like I had horns or something on my head.

I wiped my eyes, raising my hands in surrender. "I'm sorry, it's a habit I can't curb even in dreary circumstances. You will have to pardon a few slip-ups, Franklin."

"I'm starting to learn, Anne."

"Please, go on. You were saying?

"You need to make adjustments to your diet and clothing; and before you nail me to the cross for trespassing, what I mean is, eating more than you do now or at least at the right time and wearing a little less, body-fitting clothes that hugs all the right places and doesn't give you enough room to breathe. Kinda like the emerald-green gown you wore on Monday, I liked that very much," he said, avoiding my eyes.

This conversation was turning towards more

interesting grounds. So, I probed further, feigning a little annoyance.

"What I eat or wear shouldn't be of concern to you, Mr. Franklin. You're right, the girls were sensible enough not to mention it and now that you have, I can't help but feel violated."

"Liking something enough to care about them isn't a violation in my books. I was only looking out for you based on what I've seen and noticed of you. Anne, I know I might have disappeared a few times since you joined -,"

"You call not speaking to me for a full month, a few? I'm seriously wondering what a lot would be like. Maybe, I don't know, two years?

His dark eyes bored into mine as he paced the small space between our seats and the giant safe in the office, giving me room to explore his sculptured, tanned features for the first time.

He looked handsome in a suit, and even more gorgeous in a crisp white shirt, black pants, and an orange tie.

Lord help me. This man is tempting.

He stops pacing, taking his seat with sincerity in his eyes, when he said, "I like you a lot, Anne. I can't help it. When I first interrupted your meeting with the chief accountant, I thought it was just a temporary feeling or crush that would go away once we began to work together but it didn't and it scared me. That's why I haven't said more than two words to you. I figured, if

I didn't relate with you, maybe this odd feeling would go away. It hasn't."

"No."

That was the only word I could push through my tight lips.

"Excuse me?

"My answer is No, Franklin. You can save that line for any other lady of your choice, not me. Thank you for the pro tips, I'll think about considering it. If you don't mind, I've got work to do."

This time, when I felt his gaze on me after dismissing him abruptly – which came out harsher than expected – it wasn't scorching hot as expected, rather, it was warm and tender.

And that left me deeply troubled in spirit.

★★★

The pro tips worked like magic. Switching out my killer boss lady dresses for more comfortable work clothes gave me room to breathe freely and the dishes that secretly kept appearing on my desk at breakfast, lunch, and dinner time capped it all.

I was less fatigued, felt like my old self, and much more comfortable in my skin, but I wasn't excited to begin my day knowing there will always be a vacant seat at the office because apparently, spending more time in his unit was way better than the comfort of the office.

Who was I kidding? He was avoiding me after snapped at him, which equally baffled me because most men would become relentless in their pursuit and even demand to know why I didn't consider their proposal without a second thought to soothe their bruised ego.

I'll give you three reasons why.

One, I'm not interested.

Two, company policy forbids it.

Three, I simply don't give a flying fuck.

So, given that I was ardently championing the *Men are Scum campaign*, it bothered me a lot, why I kept revisiting my last conversation with Franklin. Once bitten, twice shy is the adage of old that warns about stepping into the burning fire of hurt and devastating heartbreak after it has occurred once before.

I didn't know what I expected after my outburst four days ago, but silence and free meal deliveries were the least and unexpected of them all. I was yet to figure out how to deal with my disturbing emotions as the week came to an end.

Rounding up for the day and looking forward to the weekend, I was running late with closing my accounts and asked the shuttle to go without me. I lucked out for the day by having the busiest unit in Velocity, but it didn't worry me much because I could easily book a ride home whenever I was through.

Alone and sticky, I took off my blazers and popped open the top three buttons of my shirt and relaxed to clear out the workload on my desk, hoping to leave before I got locked out of my apartment - it would be the tenth time in two months if it happened again.

With my eyes closed, I twirled to the slow blare of Adele's latest song – Send My Love to Your New Lover – with the ear pods pulled deep into my ears and the volume turned up to the highest. At this point, I could proudly say I was way past thinking about protocols, the unfinished accounts, work, rules, and any other restriction piled on top of that.

I simply got lost in the soulful beat, with rolled-up sleeves, wild, dark, pinned-down hair, and discarded shoes underneath my desk. I was the picture-perfect example of a wild child poster but that was just me, letting off steam the best way I knew.

It must have been minutes or hours later when I suddenly felt the tingling feeling at the back of my neck that I wasn't alone anymore.

My eyes flew wide open, registering the shock of seeing Franklin's amused face and followed by a hysterical scream at the poor state of my undress. My face burned red with embarrassment as his gaze dropped a notch lower from my face and remained there.

Covering my exposed bosom with both hands, I almost screamed at him. "What are you doing back here? I thought you'd left."

"I don't take the shuttle, remember? Shoot, I

forgot you didn't know much about me to know that."

"This isn't the time or place to make bad jokes, Franklin. I'm dead serious and stop laughing at me, it's not funny. You weren't supposed to see any of that. No one was."

"I guess you desperately needed the release if you forgot about that," he said pointing towards the tiny shiny camera in the room. "I might just take note of the time and ask the operator to help me search for a key or something in the morning, just to score the golden opportunity of watching the whole show again. You look wild and gorgeous, Anne. This picture of you is seared into my brain forever. Wild, Sexy, and Enthralling."

Each word that fell effortlessly from his lips turned my face a shade darker. There was no erasing that from his mind and apparently, from the database too.

Shit.

I'll blame it all on the stress and rigid environment. Yes, I think that helps. No, it doesn't. Oh, Lord!

"Hey, on a serious note, don't beat yourself up about it. There are several stupid clips of us too in the database. It's nothing to worry about as long as the big bosses don't go snooping around today's clip, which I solemnly swear won't happen. Such checks only happen when dire situations arise, which didn't," he said, trying hard and failing miserably to hide the amusement in his eyes.

He was enjoying this.

Ignoring him while I smoothed myself in place, I asked again. "You still haven't answered why you are here? You should be gone by now."

"Yes, you're right. Unfortunately, Olivia called a while ago saying she forgot her phone at the office and mentioned you were still around. So, I doubled back to get it for her," he said, stretching behind the desk to get something. "Ah–ha!" he said, shaking the phone in the air, "Got it."

"Now I know it's a habit of yours not to knock before barging in on people, I'll begin locking the doors behind me," I said, sounding defensive and slightly irritated.

He stood, towering over me and leaning in too close for comfort. "I did knock, Anne and I'm glad you didn't respond," he said, tucking a strand of loose hair behind my ears. His lean fingers trailed the side of my jaws, burning a trail down to the base of my throat.

Lifting my face to his, I could feel his breath fanning the bridge of my nose, and those tingling sensations from earlier tripled in intensity, making it difficult to get enough air down my lungs.

My body came alive with just a single touch as he transformed before me, switching from gentle to ravenously hungry.

"I don't like fighting with you and I can't seem to stay away from you either, Anne. I'm at a crossroads here and I'm teetering on the edge of two choices," he said, his voice heavily laden with sincerity and need.

"What choices are those? I asked, my voice an octave higher and sounded more like a squeak than an actual word.

"Letting you have your wish and staying away, or, showing you how I feel and risking your wrath and hate."

I blinked, digesting his words but torn even more deeply at how easy it was to connect with him. It shouldn't be this easy; falling for someone again should be so damn hard, I'd give up on the first try.

Then why do I feel so warm in his arms? Why do I want to remain here, like this, forever? Baffled and confused even more by the enigma of the man that has me hooked on his case like a crackhead on heroin, I stepped away from him, needing room to breathe.

"It's late. We should get going. Olivia won't get her phone if we keep up this staring contest and I need to get home before I get locked out of my apartment."

He sighed, sliding both hands into his pants pocket – maybe to keep from doing exactly what my mind was hoping he'd do. "At least, let me drop you off at your place. I promise not to stalk you or anything."

"I don't think –"

"And maybe come out with me this weekend for drinks. Please, it's a sincere and simple ask," he added, cutting off the refusal speech I had planned to the hilt, in half.

"Okay. One ride and One drink," I heard myself say, grabbing my things in a hurry.

So much for the leader of the *Men are Scum campaign*.

★★★

One drink, led to way too many.

I couldn't stop slugging back the shots, because in between having the best time of my life and receiving the text from that slimy bastard, I couldn't keep the emotions bottled up.

It rushed to the surface with a vengeance and wouldn't stay boxed in anymore. So consumed with trying to bury my feelings of hurt and betrayal caused by another, I was ruining the best moment of life with another.

"Talk to me, Anne, what's going on, maybe I can help? Drinking so much won't help either of us, please stop."

"Why should I trust anything you say, Frank. I trusted another and he broke my heart and almost ruined my life and career. I need more drinks."

"No, you don't, we're leaving. I made a mistake bringing you out here without giving you time to heal from your hurt."

"I didn't tell you, how – would – you – know?" I slurred, trying to get a clearer view of his face in my haze vision.

I felt hands on my waist and the next thing that

138

happened shocked me out of my slightly drunken state.

The silence that ensued proved I had done the unthinkable and the torrents poured out in earnest unaided. I couldn't believe I just hit a grown-ass man for trying to help me out.

"It's okay, Anne. Come on girl, please let's get to the car first," I heard him say, but I adamantly refuse to be led on by a lie.

"What are we even doing here, Frank? What do you hope to achieve with all this? A relationship isn't even possible between us and I'm sworn off men for good, so why do you bother and why doesn't it faze it that I'm a hot mess at the moment?

"Why should it? You have every right to be mad at me and sceptical about my moves because I know it's not my fault. This all started after you received that text and if I were to judge, I'd say it was from the bastard who hurt you in the first place."

I said nothing, too drained to form a coherent sentence without blubbering like a silly fool.

"So, I'm not bothered by the damage caused by another who doesn't know the worth of what he had; I'm concerned about the warmth and happiness I can share with you if you let me."

My emotions were all over the place and it almost felt like I was being sucked in deep. Unable to comport myself, and too embarrassed to continue with the conversation in the full glare of over fifty strangers, I grabbed my purse and left, with Franklin hot on my heels.

"Anne, wait," I heard him call out, but I furiously ploughed on, turning deaf ears to his pleading calls.

Strong arms around mine made me grind to a halt, shoving my phone in his face. "Here, that's what that sonofabitch sent to me," I said, leaving the phone with him and yanking my arms free.

I overheard him curse as I made a run for the car, seeking the sanctuary of the tainted glasses before I bawled my eyes out.

As much as it felt relieving to finally let me experience the pain of the hurt caused me, it was devastatingly more painful than I had anticipated. Too focused on leaving my past behind and getting away from Robert, I hadn't given myself to feel the full extent of his betrayal.

Now that I did, I never want to feel that way ever again.

That, and the damming implications any budding relationship between us could cause for our careers, made it extremely difficult to believe Franklin and I could ever become a real thing.

The drivers' side slid open, and he sat down, clutching my cellphone hard. "It's hard to believe there are still animals in this world, who find pleasure in hurting others. I'm sorry you ever loved someone like him."

"I'm sorry I hit you. I didn't know what came over me," I said, wiping my face, facing away from him.

He handed my phone over to me with a deep sigh. "I've never been hit by a woman before except for my mother of course. If what I just read was directed at me, I'd probably want to hit something hard too."

"How in the world are you not mad at me, after all, I just pulled? What's your restraint level, a thousand? I don't believe your calm for one minute."

Slamming his fist on the dashboard, he turned to face me with fire in his dark eyes and I jumped from his unexpected outburst. "You are right not to believe my calm because I'm mad. Scratch that, I'm furious at you for letting that sleazy ex get under your skin. I'm enraged that you don't see how beautiful you are inside and out. I'm pissed that you would want to judge your present by the hurt caused by your past."

I was taken aback by surprise at his words. Not the exact speech I was expecting.

"We might seem like an impossible pair, but I believe love blooms if given the chance to sprout. It might be slow at first, but when nurtured with patience and care, it will blossom into something beautiful."

My jaws were unhinged at this point.

"I'm not saying I love you yet, but I do know I like you enough to want to give this feeling room to sprout and blossom into something more, but as it stands, I think I should give you room to deal with your issues first. I understand now why you vehemently refused me the first time and I want you to sort through your emotions first. There is no rush."

"Franklin –," the name caught on my throat as I tried to make sense of everything happening all at once.

"Love is patient, Anne. I am a patient man and I'm here for you, always. Never forget this silent promise."

We drove to my place in silence and dropped me off without another word about the incident. I had indeed found a rare gem without seeking, and it was left for me to choose if I wanted to be ruled by hurt or love.

My phone chirped and I pulled up the new text, smiling as I read. "You are worth waiting for, Anne. You are worthy of all the love in the world," he wrote, attached with a heart emoji.

Giggling to my room, I couldn't wait to begin my new campaign, *'Give Love a Second Chance,'* you'd be surprised at what you'd find.

Obianuju Jane Ebubeoha (O.J Ebubeoha) is a Nigerian contemporary cosy romance and erotic author, with full-length novellas and several erotic series under her pen name Miss Jane.

She's a blogger, digital content creator, and accountant with an addiction to action movies and a diehard fan of gripping romance and psychological thrillers.

She's also a mental health advocate, an introvert at heart, loves nature and appreciates life.

BONUS STORY

VICIOUS CIRCLE

Agnes Kay-E

I'm in a dilemma. It was Sunday again. Barry had work, again. That was happening more often these days. Perhaps it was because I'd cleared up my Sunday schedule so we could try again. But who would blame him? He was probably feeling like a tool.

What did he expect?

He knew I had conceived once before with someone else. If I hadn't lost it, perhaps I would have had a boy, maybe a girl. Funny how *life* pokes you every so often to remind you it's watching you. Now, I've been married for eleven years, eleven months, eleven days. Ha! Imagine! It's even eleven o'clock. Life, like I said always reminds you of your misadventures… actually your inadequacies.

It was a cold and sunny day as with every spring season. I heard the horn of a car. No one living on this side of the road honked like that - like every cul-de-sac, everyone here wanted to show off their decorum, like they were dripping of it. I raised my head when I heard the crunch of pebbles. It couldn't possibly be from my neighbour's garden, which wasn't really a garden because the only thing the gnomes seemed to be doing was glare at everyone that made it to the door because there weren't flowers or greenery to protect in that garden.

I decided to feed my curiosity and make my way to the window. I pulled the blinds open and sighed heavily. I assure you; it wasn't a sigh of relief. The woman I saw was a pack of trouble, which she exuded with passion. Little wonder she wasn't married. But she did have a say in my marriage, courtesy of my husband. She was nine years his junior, four years mine, but anyone would think she was older. The good thing was, she looked it. Her name is Bose.

I hadn't set my eyes on her in close to six years, and she was coming to my house. I forgot myself for a few minutes until I heard her knock before ringing the bell. I opened the door and, as usual, she brushed past me; fortunately, her killer heels missed my foot this time. I sighed again and shut the chilly wind out. It was cold enough as it was.

I chewed my lip, wishing I had gone to church.

I watched her scan the living room to see if there was something new. Pride surged through me when she paused in front of the fifty-inch flat screen television. Yes, I bought it and everything new in the house, even though the rest was mostly from the clearance sales and the charity shop that was closing down on the high street. Her brother, my husband, had decided to go back to university for his master's degree.

That was ten months ago. Men and their timing. I

have never understood it. At the same time, the landlord sold his property and had given us two-month quit notice. He even returned our deposit with an apology. At the time, I wasn't working because my husband said I should be home to try to get pregnant. On the day of our eviction, my husband came home to tell me that he was going back to university. It was good news because I had been pleading with him to do so for years. The problem was, that he had already applied, gained admission, and registered before telling me.

Why didn't he tell me?

Was it because he was going to be studying full-time?

No.

It was because he'd used our savings to register and pay his fees. In other words, we were homeless and bankrupt.

It was like I had been left in the Alps naked. What could I do? It was his money, after all. I couldn't shout or cry. I just looked at him for a long while. The next day, I went to the café with five pounds, a few copper coins, and all my documents. I didn't know I was good at haggling until that day. I finally got my documents scanned and applied for as many vacancies as I could. I went home, sold some of my clothes to a neighbour who had always admired my taste and sent most of the rest to the charity shops close by. I saved a few as an afterthought in case I did get a job.

We moved in with his ex-girlfriend. I think that was what really brought tears to my eyes. I had always assumed she was a family friend. She was working full-time, of course. He and she had agreed that I would take care of her eighteen-month-old child, without asking me first. He mentioned it in passing and I pretended not to hear him, but when I heard the baby crying and noticed they had already left the house, what else could I do?

Two weeks after we moved in with his ex-girlfriend, I went to the garden to bask in the sunlight and saw a woman struggling with her kids and was able to calm them. I didn't know she had postpartum depression. I didn't even know such a thing existed.

Her husband came knocking the following day and asked me if I could help them from time to time until his mother came in from Australia. Of course, I agreed. I was bored. Two weeks later, he gave me an envelope and introduced me to his mother. When I got home, I opened the envelope and saw it was money. I broke down, and though I cried, I was elated. It was my first salary ever. I had missed so many interviews because I didn't have travel money. So, I was surprised to receive a call for an interview I had missed, they were apologizing for cancelling the interview without a heads up. Imagine that!

I used half of the money to hire someone to look after the ex's child and told her that I had employed the woman for only four weeks. I would never forget the look on her face but was disgusted by the smug look on my husband's face.

Why was he feeling smug? He couldn't even defend my cooking whenever she condemned my food. I decided to stop cooking. When she cooked…

He started eating at his best friends, Warren and Etido's house. They were brothers. He had been eating there since then. Warren was finally relocating to Nigeria, as he and his wife had gotten lucrative jobs simultaneously. It was only then that they knew I could be useful. For one, his wife had developed amnesia after calling me a 'witch' and accusing me of using charms to prevent Barry from marrying his ex-girlfriend, her cousin with a 'perfectly formed womb' from a 'family of fertile women'.

My family had fertile women too. I got married six years before my sisters, and they all had more than one child; sometimes they slighted me too.

Sometimes fate smiles on you too. Well, that's how I started working with the NHS. A few months before, an ex-boyfriend, my first love and first crush, had died and left me a lot of money. Meanwhile, my godfather, who happened to be Barry's uncle, gave me a lot of money. So, before my husband could come up with a pansy scheme, I bought a house. Do you know what it means to live rent-free, mortgage-free in England? At the budding age of thirty-seven? Of course, for all intents and purposes, all the money came from my godfather.

I had generally stopped going to parties because where one set of people showered me with pity, the other sect showered me with furtive glances of suspicion. If they even talked to me, it was centred around McD, how easy or difficult it was to poop the baby, potty-training, and of course, if the tooth fairy should be kept real and for how long and for that I had a scantily clad wardrobe. A fashionista like me.

Life.

★★★

I sigh and observe Bose. Bose's visit is for a few days, I hoped. Barry's shift finishes at seven that evening and Bose was about to be hit by a surprise. I smirked. Dropping by unannounced after so many years? She'd better call her brother to feed her. As if in her defence, my stomach rumbled. I grimaced coyly, I was going to finish anything I ordered from the Chinese restaurant, which meant I'd have to order something I could finish; that was an exam in itself. I racked my brain, wondering where I last saw the take-out flyer. Then I remembered where it was and headed for the bedroom.

As I climbed the steps, I heard clashing and clanking. I'd been meaning to replace those pots since we got married. I shook my head and continued to my room. It was the only room that'd been furnished.

Fortunately, the others were carpeted, and both had mattresses on the ground, so she would be able to manage. As I reached my room, I suddenly felt exhausted and plopped on the bed staring at the ceiling. It seemed interesting. White. There was a time in my life that I always wore white.

I hear Bose's footsteps and roll my eyes. Picking up the phone, I called the restaurant, placed my order, and then picked up my wallet. As I make to remove some money from it, I recall how Bose always went through Barry's things and mine and emptied it – I never told him. Ha! How do you possibly tell your husband that his only sister pilfers? No, *takes*. Perhaps he knew or maybe he suspected me. Anyway, as a precaution, I emptied my wallet and headed downstairs.

She met me at the landing and rolled her eyes at me. I shrugged because I was more concerned with my order. The doorbell chimed just as I was about to sit down.

That was fast, I thought. I did what I normally didn't do. I opened the door before seeing who it was. Lo and behold, it was Doctor Gbenró Oreju. I gulped and choked, and I couldn't clear my throat because it was embarrassing to see him standing tall with his imposing ebony frame in my doorway.

Doctor Oreju was my office crush who was too keen where I was concerned. My chest felt as if it was on fire, so I quickly gestured for him to go in.

He took my cue and walked in while I walked onto the porch. The winter wind calmed my nerves, and I went back in. Small world. I didn't know he knew Bose. He was one of the few doctors that left his patients smiling at the end of their visit.

I turned around when I heard a car rev, but I still waited because I could hear a scooter from a distance. A tall lanky man with dreadlocks and dressed as a Rastafarian got off. I blinked when it occurred to me that he was heading in my direction. He looked scruffy but smelt clean. He mumbled a greeting.

"I'll take it from here," Bose said, rolling her eyes, and nudging me back with her shoulder so that she ended up between me and Rastafarian.

I raised my hands in surrender and relief.

She threw herself on him and all I could see were the moulds of her buttocks in his firm grip.

"Let's go," Bose muttered.

I turned to the door and remembered Bose's guest then turn to remind her and saw her shove Rastafarian off the porch. She turned around and mouthed, "Don't tell Gbenró." Then she shouted, "Don't wait up!"

I blinked in surprise and confusion.

"Hello, ma'am," a bald man whisked me out of my thought.

"Oh, hello," I replied. My food had been delivered.

"I think I lost patron of you," The bald man said as I gave him his money.

I smiled at him. I'd always known he wasn't

Chinese; he was Malaysian and could speak Cantonese.

"I've been busy." See, these three words, work like magic in this country. I don't know how the excuse started, but God bless them, honestly. We made the exchange, and I closed the door behind me.

"Bose…" Dr Oreju started.

"You just missed her," I said, setting the bags down so I can pick my ringing phone.

He leaned back and crossed one leg over the other. "Oh, I'll wait for her."

Amused, I glared at him.

"Don't give me that look! She said she was only going to the convenience store uphill." He adjusted his shirt and added, "She won't be long."

"I'm afraid she isn't coming back tonight," I mumbled and press the green button on my phone.

He chuckled. I thought he didn't believe me because he sat so comfortably, quite arrogantly too. I didn't know if I should be offended or amused.

"Hello," I coo into my phone.

"Hello? Na wa o!"

"I didn't —"

"Anyway, I can't make it home today. I have to leave for Scotland right away. Egbon has already paid for my flight. I'll explain when I get back."

The line went dead. I blinked and frowned at my phone. Who was Egbon? Because anytime he pulled this Egbon stunt, he doesn't return for at least three to four days. Tomorrow was a bank holiday, and I was ovulating. Sometimes I wondered if he doesn't want me to have his child.

It's funny how you could actually love someone and despise them at the same time. I mean it; I didn't know it was possible. I loved my husband to bits, but I most certainly wouldn't die for him, not then anyway. I remembered when we first met; I was in front of hostel C on my university campus, trying to prevent a classmate of mine from fighting with her drunk boyfriend. He applauded his friend's staggering stance. I rebuked him and he simply smiled and walked away. I later found out he was the teaching assistant to one of my lecturers in my most difficult course.

I slanted my head to the side so Doctor Oreju didn't see me cry and at the same time, tried to compose myself in a delightful manner. Then my eyes fell on the wine cabinet. I walked briskly to the cabinet before I lost the courage. Since I wasn't one for drinking alone, I went to the kitchen without asking him and brought back two glasses and plates for the food. He accepted them without question. It was then that I saw his face; he looked so crestfallen, I almost pitied him.

He ate his food quietly. I did have to say, he was polite or perhaps humbled. Suddenly, he looked like a blurry spectre.

I squinted then sniffled and knew I was in my stealth sobbing mode. First, my husband was being the man he was, everywhere else but home, while Bose had come to steal the little peace I had and now I was seeing things? I closed my eyes to fight back the tears and leaned back on the sofa.

The scent of Dr Oreju's perfume jarred my thought, and I opened my eyes. I watched his arms reach for me and didn't stop it from being wrapped around me. Not realising how much I missed human contact I broke down. I knew I shouldn't let him hold me anymore, but a few minutes wouldn't hurt. Perhaps when I finished bawling.

The thought of human contact intensified my unrestrained sobs. I snuggled in, even more, when he began to rub my back to soothe me and pulled me closer. He cooed into my ear then his hand brushed my breast and my nipple tingled. I decided that the world could wait.

Something had changed because the person moaning was me. There were no warning bells except the one between Dr Oreju's thighs. His hand resting below my midriff and my nipple in his mouth held a promise I just couldn't resist. The world must wait, I thought, then surrendered to the pleasure I've been longing for.

★★★

It had been four months now and fortunately; I was no longer nauseous from whatever stomach bug I may have had. I knew I was supposed to get it checked out, but I hated needles and still do. Angela, a doctor at the surgery I worked in, commented on the zits that had begun to leisurely crowd my face. I was beginning to feel dizzy again and this time Angela caught me. She asked me into her office.

"Lie down," she ordered as she slipped her hands into her surgical gloves.

Neat freak! Which she was, but my heart skipped at the same time. I had never liked hospitals and worse still injections. "I'm alright, Angie."

"Right now, I'm your doctor."

"Yes, ma'am." I climbed onto the examination table and lay down. That position seemed to calm my aching head. "What is this about?"

"Raise your blouse quickly." Angela impatiently stood there with her hands raised. I didn't have an appointment and she had a patient in five minutes.

"My doctor isn't rude," I muttered and did as I was told. I could indulge her if only to rest my head for a bit.

She started her checks and when she got to my lower abdomen, I winced. She left and came back. "Pee in this."

I grimaced.

"Go on."

I snatched the small bottle, but she smiled sweetly irritating me even more. To get back at her, I didn't clean the outside of the bottle after peeing in it. I smirked when I returned. I'd forgotten she was wearing gloves.

Taking it, she unscrewed the top and dipped a strip in it. "How have you been feeling lately?"

"Like a truck rolled over me."

"You wouldn't survive that."

I rolled my eyes. That was Angela alright; moulded in logic - no sarcasm, no sense of humour. She was the best doctor in this surgery. You know what they say about 'our brains making up for what we don't have'.

Angela cleared her throat.

I tilted my head up to see her smiling. "What is it?" I snapped. I was definitely irritated; the worst part was I couldn't understand why.

"You're pregnant!" She came and hugged me. "Congratulations! Ah yes, no more coffee for you."

I stared at her, dumbfounded. I pushed her off and grimaced. Pregnant? How? We'd been trying for a long time, but recently, Barry was never there for us to try. As I stepped out of her office, I bumped into Dr Oreju.

An awkward silence ensued, then he cleared his throat.

"I'm sorry, I wasn't watching," I said and briskly walked away.

"Are you alright?" he asked, but I ignored him.

I hadn't seen him since that day in my sitting room. I knew he was away with a few of his friends for Doctors without Borders − courtesy of office gossip. He did smell nice. I rushed to the loo and puked my guts out. My heart was in reflux just as a large burp escaped my mouth. Seeing him reminded me of my sin. I held my stomach and remembered Angela's news.

What if… no, it could never be. It could never be! God forbid! What would I tell the world? I reject it, in Jesus' name! Amen! It was definitely not his.

I'm pregnant. I'm pregnant! Wow, after all these years.

★★★

I groaned inwardly as I looked at the computer screen.

"I'm sorry when did you say you booked your appointment?"

A girl with pink braids and a freckled face appeared over the old woman's shoulder. "I forgot to book your appointment. I'm sorry, Naan," she said, trying to get the woman's attention.

You know the feeling you get when you're caressed by a gentle breeze on a very hot day? That's how I felt when I heard that. Mrs Callaghan had Alzheimer's. Was it wrong to want to secure my job?

"Is it possible to see Dr Oreju, please?" the girl in pink braids asked, her face turning red as she did.

Hearing his name made me shiver. To be honest, I couldn't tell if it was from trepidation or excitement. "Of course, please take a seat." I coughed to remove the tremor in my voice and quickly typed in her name. Most doctors would stand by their doors to welcome their patients into their daunting rooms, but not Dr Oreju. He came out and as if to remind me of my guilt, he lingered. The pink-braided girl turned purple on seeing him. He let them walk ahead of him before he looked at me with a smug smile on his face. I quickly looked away and tried to bring my shaking hands under control. I just need to be sure of the paternity or I'd be doomed.

★★★

Weeks turned to months, and I still hadn't told my husband I was pregnant. Anytime I thought of telling him, the ground seemed to cave in. He was going to find out very soon, and by my calculations, it wasn't his. What was he going to do to me when he found out? I was beginning to show. God help me. I was going to tell him right after a nap, which will probably be my last, so I clocked out early.

It was quiet when I got home. Unfortunately, my usually absentee husband was home. He looked crestfallen. Even though he has spent most of our marriage annoying me, I still yearned for him, so I went to him and rubbed his back to soothe him.

"What is it?" I asked, genuinely concerned.

"I thought he was mine," Barry murmured more to himself.

I frowned. Who was his? I had long since learnt to keep quiet and listen because it was at times like these that my husband revealed the deep and secret things that haunted him.

"She said he was mine. Why did she put me through this?"

"Who? What are you talking about?" I asked before I could stop myself and gritted my teeth. How pathetic. I just shut the door on my thumb!

"What?" Barry asked, suddenly aware of what he was doing. With the audacity of a straight face, he asked, "When did you get back?"

"I just did," I retorted through clenched teeth.

He exhaled heavily.

It was no use admitting defeat. I got up, folded my arms and glared at him.

"Honey, I'm sorry, I've had a lot on my mind. My dissertation is giving me stress and –"

"Save it." I usually used these scenarios to my advantage, but my mind was in tatters already. 'She said he was mine' was definitely about a child, right? So, he has been cheating on me.

'Well, no one will accuse me of being barren,' I

almost blurt out.

To save myself from my mouth, I left him and went upstairs. On climbing the stairs, I heard water trickling and groaned. I had almost forgotten that Bose was still in the house, as we barely saw each other.

As I turned off the tap, I thought of taking a long bath and looked for the bath soap. I found it, plugged the tub, turned the tap on and went to my room. All the while, I was thinking of how I was going to tell my husband. Feeling lightheaded, I lay down briefly.

I walked morosely to the bath. I dipped myself in the warm water and sighed. A few minutes later, I felt something cold on my face and opened my eyes. My husband was kneeling by the bath, playing with the water, and letting his hand slide all over me. I moaned as he made his way down and then paused on my stomach. I cringed and stayed still, waiting.

He murmured in my ear and I gradually relaxed.

I frowned when I no longer felt his hand on me. A few seconds had passed, so I cracked my eyes open to see that he wasn't there. The next second, I felt his hands on my neck and my world came to an end...

"Wow, you're so tense!" he said as he began to knead the nape of my neck.

I figured I could tell him then and I did, but not properly, as I blurted out, "I'm four months pregnant." I smiled with relief and looked at him. It was the way that he was looking at me that made me wonder what I had done wrong. "I..," I said, trying to salvage the situation, but it was too late. His hands were curled around my neck in a tight grip, so tight that I couldn't even squeak. I pleaded with my eyes and dug my nails in his hand…

I woke with my hands on my neck. I shuddered as I recalled the nightmare. Shaking my head, I plumped a pillow and lay back down.

I sat up just as my eyes fell on the blue satin blanket. I had never liked blue. It was Barry's favourite colour. I rushed to the kitchen to check on the dinner roasting in the oven. He had submitted his dissertation and was home early the first time in a long time.

He ogled me, looked at my body and smiled. My breast size had significantly increased. I winked at him and smiled then showed him a letter to prove I was pregnant just like they did in Nigerian movies. He got excited and asked me how long. I told him and the next thing I knew. I was on the ground in a foetal position, and he was raining abuses on me and asking who's the pregnancy was. I stared at him my mind completely blank. I felt my chest constrict as he fisted his hands and walked toward me.

I woke up with a shriek.

I had never had a nightmare in my life. But two? Remembering the superstition, I knocked on the bedside table. I'm not superstitious, but I'd rather not find out what the consequences were. Then I realised how stupid it was to knock on wood in the first place, as the nightmare had already taken place. I sat up, glad that the headache was gone. The nightmare replayed in my mind.

If I told him in Nigeria, Barry would probably pummel me into mincemeat and call my family to come and take me. But here? He would kill me and turn me into chopsticks so no one would find me. I was already known as a loner. The only people I had been in constant relation with were the staff at the surgery. I couldn't continue like this. This was a mental breakdown in the preface. I figured I had a few choices: tell my husband, but first, get the police on speed dial, or call everyone I knew in Nigeria but not wait to speak to them, so they'd be forced to call me back, then tell him. I opted for choice two. I topped up on my phone data online and called everyone as planned. Some were rather quick to pick up the calls, so in those instances, I made up an excuse that would cause them to call me back.

I ran down the stairs, pausing on the last one to catch my breath. I heard hurried steps and just before the front door opened and closed, I heard Bose cry, "I'll see you people next week." in Yoruba.

The door slamming shut hitched my racing heart.

I peered into the kitchen when I reach it and saw Barry. This was it then. I exhaled. He had a knife in his hand and turned to look at me. I raised a brow and cleared my throat, more like coughed.

"Do you want some?" he asked, gesturing at the

apples on the table.

I shrugged. My heart had constricted, and my throat was dry, but I moved closer. How else was I going to take the knife off him?

"Well, here." He handed me the knife. "Help yourself."

I sliced the apple slowly, taking surreptitious glances at him.

He frowned. "Are you okay?"

I nodded, my legs now jelly.

He shrugged and leaned forward. "Maybe I should help you with those."

"Oh no, no, no, I'm fine. It's okay, see?" I squeaked and tried to smile and cut quickly so quickly that the knife pierced my finger.

"Look at what you've done. Give me the knife."

"No," I shouted.

"I'll slice the apples for you, just clean the wound."

My thoughts were centred on 'give me the knife', 'I'll slice' and the pain I felt when the knife pierced my skin. I tossed the knife in the sink instead and hurried to it. My chest was on fire, breathing became more difficult than ever before.

Shaking his head, Barry left the kitchen to my relief.

I let the cold water wash and cool my hand but I couldn't stand anymore, so I knelt down by the sink and prayed.

"Oh God! Please make it quick and painless," I continued to mutter. I needed it to be over and done with, so I walked back to the sitting room, picked up the remote control and pressed the mute button.

My breathing was far quicker than that of the women I had seen in labour. As I sat down, I had to hunch my back to ease the pain. "I need to tell you something."

Barry thinned his lips and leaned back on the settee. "Obviously."

"I'm pregnant!" I whispered and the soles of my feet became unbearably hot. I kicked off my slippers and began to pace.

"It's not yours. I swear it only happened once! In a dazed drunken moment." I wanted to say more, but words were not coming out of my mouth. They seemed to have deserted me. Who could blame them? Perhaps words could be murdered too. In my head, I began to chant: *Painless and quick, painless and quick.*

I looked at him. My vision was blurry through my tears, but I could still see him sitting down with his arms crossed. I waited a long time but was taken aback when he finally walked to the wine cabinet, poured himself a shot, and returned to his seat.

I stopped pacing and watched him gulp it and look straight at me as he said, "Well, it's the only chance of our having children. Therefore, you can't get rid of it."

Life and its curveballs, eh?

Agnes Kay-E is a Nigerian author based in England and the author of eight books, including Blossom in Winter, a bestseller. She writes contemporary women's fiction, fantasy, and new-age fiction. Her latest is Cursed Blossoms. She is presently working on another contemporary fiction book. In her spare time, she sings and writes music.

OTHER KEPRESSNG ANTHOLOGIES

Ogu & Other Stories

Rebirth

Flip-Flop

Oops!

Bound by Fate

Sink or Swim

Loving Nigeria

CONTACTS

Thank you for purchasing this book.
I hope you enjoyed it.

Please leave a review of what you thought of this book at your favourite retailer.

For more, let's meet at any of these places.

Facebook: https://www.facebook.com/kepressng
Instagram: https://www.instagram.com/kepressng
For newsletters: https://www.kepressng.com

ABOUT US

Kemka Ezinwo Press (KEP) Ltd is an African publishing company with the vision of broadening the power of African literary works and compositions. Our aim is to remind the world that we're avid readers, and to combat the self-imposed superstitions that Africans don't read.

Our core values are Excellence, Collaboration, Discovery, & Generosity.

To launch our official opening, we decided to introduce the KepressNG Anthology prize, a collection of shorts from debut and veteran authors with African lineage multi-collection. We incorporated our Vision of developing and increasing African literature by making it a competition for the selection of the best story.

The KepressNG Anthology prize is designed for teenagers, though not restricted to them, to write stories that they'd hope to read. Our stories matter, and who better than us to tell our stories? Societies change and the most affected are the young.

The idea of tying the story to a theme is our way of helping new and emerging authors establish a discipline of telling us the story without the faff.

The prose is in short form and not restricted to a specific genre.

There's a belief that short stories are a thing of the past but most young adults start out with short stories. Should we now abandon them in the abyss and anarchy of their literary formation proficiency?

As an anthology prize giver, we want to rebuild and reinstate the idea that writing is lucrative if only to the individual's aesthetics, thereby building better mental health and expanding knowledge.